CHRIS RYAN

UNDER COVER

RED FOX

*Available by Chris Ryan and
published by Random House Children's Publishers UK:*

The One That Got Away

AGENT 21 series
Agent 21
Agent 21: Reloaded
Agent 21: Codebreaker
Deadfall

CODE RED series
Flash Flood
Wildfire
Outbreak
Vortex
Twister
Battleground

ALPHA FORCE series
Survival
Rat-Catcher
Desert
Pursuit
Hostage
Red Centre
Hunted
Blood Money
Fault Line
Black Gold
Untouchable

Published by the Random House Group for adult readers:

NON-FICTION
The One That Got Away
Chris Ryan's SAS Fitness Book
Chris Ryan's Ultimate Survival Guide
Fight to Win: Deadly Skills of the Elite Forces

FICTION
Stand By, Stand By
Zero Option
The Kremlin Device
Tenth Man Down
Hit List
The Watchman
Land of Fire
Greed
The Increment
Blackout
Ultimate Weapon
Strike Back
Firefight
Who Dares Wins
One Good Turn (Adult Quick Read for World Book Day 2008)

UNDER COVER

UNDER COVER
A RED FOX BOOK 978 1 849 41011 3

Published in Great Britain by Red Fox,
an imprint of Random House Children's Publishers UK
A Penguin Random House Company

This edition published 2015

7 9 10 8

Copyright © Chris Ryan, 2015
Cover artwork © Stephen Mulcahey
Photography © Jonny Ring

Penguin Random House is committed to a sustainable future for our business, our readers and our planet.
This book is made from Forest Stewardship Council® certified paper.

Typeset in Adobe Garamond by Falcon Oast Graphic Art Ltd.

Corgi Books are published by Random House Children's Publishers UK,
61–63 Uxbridge Road, London W5 5SA

www.**randomhousechildrens**.co.uk
www.**totallyrandombooks**.co.uk
www.**randomhouse**.co.uk

Addresses for companies within The Random House Group Limited
can be found at: www.randomhouse.co.uk/offices.htm

THE RANDOM HOUSE GROUP Limited Reg. No. 954009

A CIP catalogue record for this book is available from the British Library.

Printed and bound in Great Britain by Clays Ltd, Elcograf S.p.A.

CONTENTS

PART ONE

1

THROWN AWAY

Trafalgar Square, London
Thursday, 11:30 a.m.

Police!

How many?

Two on the north side, three on the south.

Are they going to be a problem?

I hope not. We'll keep an eye on them. If they look like causing trouble, we'll move somewhere else.

But Ricky Mahoney didn't want to move anywhere else. This was the best place in London for what he had in mind.

Ricky wasn't like other fourteen-year-old kids. It wasn't just the scruffy clothes or the second-hand trainers with the holes in them that made him different. It wasn't just that he had spent the past year and a half living by himself, with no adults, in a sordid room in an overcrowded, falling-down old

Victorian house in north-east London. It wasn't just that, by his own admission, he was a sneak, a pick-pocket and a thief.

It was his habit of talking to himself that made Ricky think he was *really* weird. All day he discussed things in his head with an imaginary accomplice called Ziggy. Totally crazy, but Ricky didn't care. Because when you don't have any real friends, some-times imaginary ones will do just as well.

Ziggy was an argumentative so-and-so. Right now he was picking apart one of Ricky's little lessons in the finer points of petty crime.

– *It's the ones with the phones that get me*, Ricky said. He never spoke to Ziggy out loud. Their conversations always took place in his head.

– *What do you mean? What's wrong with them?*

Ricky never carried a phone. He had no need for it. If he ever managed to steal a decent one, though, he knew a place in the East End where he could sell it for up to fifty quid. So he always found it a bit weird how everyone else was so obsessed with them.

– *Well, how many people can we see? Five hundred? And half of them are staring at their screens or taking selfies. Seriously, I could pick the pocket of any one of them, easy as falling off a log.*

– *Then why don't you do it? Your rent's due tomorrow, and we haven't eaten for two days.*

Good point. Ricky's stomach rumbled. He needed a meal.

He was leaning against one of the stone lions in Trafalgar Square, having worked out ages ago that this was a good place to be invisible. Invisible was how he liked to be. Invisible was good for a pick-pocket. There were loads of other young people there. Some of them were splashing in the fountains. Some were chasing pigeons across the square. Others were kicking their heels behind their mum and dad as if they were in the middle of the world's most boring day. Nobody would ever notice just one more kid loitering by the lions.

Trafalgar Square had another advantage. There were *always* tourists there. Packs of them, staring up to the top of Nelson's Column and barely paying any attention to what was going on around them. These tourists were easy pickings. They were like walking cash machines where you didn't even need to use a cash card to withdraw your money.

– *Hold up. Who's that?*

– *Where?*

– *Over there. North side of the square. A couple of Thrownaways.*

'Thrownaways' was the word Ricky used for the homeless kids who worked the streets of London. They were everywhere, if you just opened your eyes and looked – which most people didn't, of course. At night they met in the dingier parts of King's Cross or under the bridges that spanned the Thames. The Thrownaways were a rough bunch who congregated in gangs, which could be aggressive and violent – Ricky kept his distance. He'd only ever had one proper encounter with them. He glanced down at the wrist of his left hand to see a pale white scar following the line of his arm. It was a reminder of how that little encounter had ended badly for him.

He squinted as he looked across the square. A girl about his own age was standing half a metre behind a Japanese man taking a photo of his girlfriend. A boy was walking swiftly in her direction. He'd be next to her in about five seconds. They made momentary eye contact.

– *Watch this. Oldest technique in the book.*

The girl stretched out her left hand. She slipped it into the side pocket of the Japanese man's linen jacket. When she removed it, she was carrying something. A wallet. It all happened very quickly, like the flicking of a gecko's tongue.

Now the boy was right behind her, still walking. Even Ricky couldn't see the moment when the wallet changed hands. The boy disappeared into the crowd. For all Ricky knew, he'd already handed the wallet to a third accomplice. A few seconds later, the Japanese man was asking the girl to take a photo of him and his girlfriend. She agreed with a smile.

– *Quite nicely done*, Ricky thought grudgingly.

– *You could join the Thrownaways if you wanted, you know. Get someone to work as your partner. It's safer that way.*

– *Well, I don't want to. If we had a partner, they'd grass us up if things got tricky. The do-gooders would have their hands on us before we knew it.*

And anyway, Ricky thought, he hadn't been 'thrown away' in the first place. He'd left home – if you wanted to call it that – of his own accord. And he wasn't a street kid, exactly. He wasn't living in a doorway or a cardboard box, or under a bridge, or even in a hostel. He had a place to stay. In his position, little things like that made a difference. It was a question of pride – even if it did mean having old Baxter as a landlord.

He continued to scan the crowd and ignored the gnawing hunger in the pit of his stomach. Ziggy was right. Today was Thursday. He hadn't eaten since Tuesday lunch time. It wasn't that he hadn't been busy. Far from it. He'd grabbed three wallets since then. Forty pounds in the first, twenty in the second and fifty in the third. A good haul, but not enough yet to pay his monthly rent to old Baxter. Ricky's vile landlord would be round for his money tomorrow evening, which meant Ricky had to turn at least one more trick. Especially if he also wanted to eat.

He picked out a couple of possibles. There was a mum pushing her kid in a pushchair. Ricky never pickpocketed young mums. It didn't seem fair, somehow. His eyes picked out a harassed-looking teacher with a bunch of school kids. No way. The teacher wouldn't be a problem, but Ricky knew that children were more observant than adults. They saw everything.

– *So just go for one of the idiots looking at their phones*, Ziggy suggested, *if they're so easy.*

– *Nah. Like shooting fish in a barrel. Got to keep your skills fresh.*

– *Oh, come on, Ricky. You must have stolen two hundred wallets in your time. You've never been caught.*

– *Yeah. Because I keep my skills fresh.*

He continued to scan the crowds. A few seconds later, his eyes locked onto a man walking towards Nelson's Column from the north-west corner of the square. He was tall, with broad shoulders. A black guy, his head was bald and shiny, and he wore a blue cagoule, even though there was no sign of rain. He seemed to be sweating a lot – as he walked, he patted his bald pate with a handkerchief. What was more important, the cagoule was flapping open, its unzipped outer pockets clearly visible, a map of the tube sticking out of the man's trouser pocket.

– *A tourist*, Ricky thought. He bent down and undid the lace of his right shoe. Then he jumped down from the plinth on which the stone lion sat. He walked twenty paces north before turning ninety degrees to the right. Ten paces, he reckoned, before his path crossed his target's. He watched the man out of the corner of his eye, and even from a distance he could tell where the wallet was – the right-hand pocket of the man's cagoule was slightly weighted down, as though it contained something heavy. In Ricky's line of work, heavy wallets were the best kind. He also saw something he hadn't noticed from his vantage point on the plinth. The man had a stout walking stick in his right hand, and walked with a slight limp.

Five paces.

– *Here goes.*

Ricky was a metre away from the man when he 'tripped' over his undone shoelace. It was, he thought, quite an impressive fall – one that he had practised in private probably a hundred times until he could do it without hurting himself. But now, splayed on the hard ground directly in front of the man's feet, he screwed up his face in pain and started to shake.

The man stopped. He looked down at the figure sprawled at his feet. 'What the hell's this?' he said. 'Are you auditioning for Coco the Clown?' He sounded like he had something in his mouth, and Ricky realized he was sucking a sweet.

'*Ow!*' Ricky wiped away a non-existent tear with the back of his left hand. He held his hand up, so the man could pull him to his feet. The man peered at him. He looked slightly amused.

– *Don't do it*, Ziggy warned. *Don't pick his pocket. This one's not as stupid as he looks.*

– *It'll be fine.*

A weighty wallet was worth a bit of risk.

Ricky staggered up. As he did so, he slipped his right hand into the man's cagoule pocket. Sure enough, there was a fat wallet hiding inside.

– *There you go. Easy as falling off a—*

'You should do your laces up, Coco,' the man said.

'Yeah,' Ricky said, looking directly into the man's eyes to stop his target's gaze from wandering. The man returned the stare with a strange sort of half-smile.

'Probably.' He had the wallet in his fist now. It felt good and heavy. He slipped it up into his right-hand sleeve where he had sewn a little pocket.

– *Job done.*

'Unless you're planning another pratfall sometime soon.'

Ricky hesitated, just for a moment.

– *He knows you were faking it.*

– *No he doesn't. He's just a weirdo who wants to chat.*

But Ricky did feel a little uneasy as he got down onto one knee and started doing up the lace. The man was standing over him.

'Would you like a sweet?' the man asked. 'I've got some here somewhere.' He started patting down his cagoule with his free hand.

'No, really,' said Ricky as the man's hands drifted alarmingly close to the pocket that had once held his wallet. 'I . . . I don't really eat sweets.'

The man blinked in surprise. 'Weird,' he murmured. 'Still, if you're sure.'

'Quite sure, thanks.'

'OK. No sweets. But there is one other thing.'

'What?'

'You should probably give me my wallet back.'

Ricky froze. His laces were still undone as he got to his feet. 'I don't know what you—'

'It's up your right sleeve. Just in case you've forgotten.' The man grinned, and Ricky saw a mouthful of yellowing and rotten teeth. 'Happens to the best of us.'

Ricky sized the man up. He was tall and looked strong, but there *was* that walking stick, not to mention the limp. Ricky, on the other hand, was thin and gangly. A bit of a weakling. Rubbish at fighting.

But fast.

And he knew that sometimes you have to play to your strengths.

His mouth was dry. His heart was pumping.

– *Run!* said Ziggy.

Ricky ran.

2

THE CHUCKLE BROTHERS

Crowds, Ricky had noticed, always seem busier when you're trying to escape them. He felt his loose shoelaces whipping round his ankles as he swerved at top speed around the tourists. His pulse was racing as he approached the busy road circling Trafalgar Square.

– *Mind the cars!* Ziggy screamed.

The road was crammed full of buses, black cabs and other vehicles. A couple of them sounded their horn furiously as Ricky sprinted across the road towards the Strand, dodging the moving cars as he went.

He was sweating heavily by the time he made it safely to the other side. He allowed himself a moment to look over his shoulder.

The man was standing on the edge of Trafalgar

Square. He didn't look flustered. In fact, he still had that slightly amused look on his face as he stared directly at Ricky.

– He makes me nervous.

– Me too.

– You couldn't fool him.

– Thanks for the reminder.

– Maybe your skills aren't so awesome after all.

– Shut up, Ziggy.

Ricky looked forward and started running again, east along the Strand.

He figured that anyone in pursuit would expect him to head north and get lost in the side streets of Covent Garden. But there was a little shortcut he knew – some steps that headed south off the Strand towards the river. He stopped at the top of them and looked back again. No sign of the man. With a limp and a walking stick he wouldn't be moving fast – unless he was good at hopping. Ricky descended two steps at a time. At the bottom, he stopped to regain his breath and tie his shoelaces, his back against a brick wall.

– Relax!

– I'm trying . . .

His hands were trembling. He'd come so close to being caught, and he knew what *that* would mean. A march down to the police station, and before he knew it he'd be back in care. The do-gooders would have him in their clutches, good and proper.

– *What's in the wallet?*

Still crouching down after tying his laces, Ricky removed the wallet from his sleeve and opened it up. He grinned. It was stuffed full of notes. He reckoned there were several hundred pounds in there. There were also nine or ten credit cards. Ricky pulled a couple of cards out and immediately saw that they had different names on them: R. F. E. Martin and Mr Jim Daniels. He flicked through some more of the cards. Dr H. Newland. Mr Godfrey S. Davies. There was a driving licence and a library card, both with a photo of the man – the black skin, the bald head – but each with a different name.

– *What is he? Some sort of criminal? A fraudster?*

– *You've messed with the wrong guy.*

Ricky tucked the cards back into the wallet. He wouldn't try to use any of them. If the police were after this guy, they'd be monitoring his cards and that would be a great way to lead them to Ricky. The cash, though, was a different matter – completely untraceable. Ricky tucked the wallet into his pocket. He was already imagining the food he'd buy with it. A burger, maybe. Extra fries. Large milkshake . . .

'Are you sure you won't have a sweet, Coco?'

Ricky's blood froze as a shadow fell over him. A

metre away he saw two feet and the bottom of a walking stick. He looked up.

The man still had a slight smile. But there was a hint of steel in his eyes.

– He's bad news. All those identities, could be organized crime. You don't want to get mixed up in that. Just give him the wallet and get out of here.

Ricky eased himself to his feet. He removed the wallet from his pocket and handed it over.

'Thank you very much,' said the man in his deep voice. 'I'm wondering if you happened to take a look inside?'

Ricky shook his head.

'Names,' the man continued, obviously not believing him. 'Some are more suitable than others for different occasions. What's *your* name, by the way?'

'Billy,' Ricky lied instinctively.

The man looked delighted. 'You see how easy it is! Now you have three names – Billy, Coco and whatever your real one is.'

'Right,' Ricky said. Today was getting weirder by the second. So was this bloke. 'Er, are you going to tell the police about me?'

'The police? God, no. They can be very tiresome at times.' He pulled a twenty-pound note from his wallet. 'Are you hungry?' he said.

Ricky couldn't help but nod.

'Me too. So why don't I buy you something to eat, and I can tell you where you went wrong?'

Something to eat. Ricky salivated at the thought.

– *Don't be stupid*, Ziggy told him. *This guy's trouble. Smile sweetly and get out of here.*

Ricky edged along the wall, back towards the steps. The man gave a little shrug and offered him the twenty-pound note anyway. Uncertainly, Ricky took it. But the moment the man released it from his fingers, he grabbed Ricky's wrist. It was a tight grip, and made Ricky wince.

'Every lie needs an element of truth, Coco,' the man said. 'Next time you try the pratfall, make sure there's some blood. Knee, elbow, anywhere. Use the fake stuff if you have it, it's pretty good. If I'd seen that, you might have got away with it.'

'Let go of me.'

'And when you know you're faster than someone, run in a straight line. Otherwise they might out-think you, like I just did. And you've got to admit, it's a bit embarrassing being caught by a man with only one leg.'

'*What?*'

The man released his grip and Ricky staggered towards the steps.

'Afraid so,' the man said. He tapped the lower

half of his leg with his stick. It made a dull, clunk-ing sound.

– *Good skills*, Ziggy said slyly. *Outrun by a bloke with one—*

– *Shut up, Ziggy.*

Now Ricky really wanted to get out of there.

'Tell me, Coco.'

'What?'

The man smiled, once more revealing the teeth of a man who ate more sweets than was good for him. 'Do you want a job?'

– *A job? What sort of job would a guy like him be offering?*

'Course not,' he said.

'Oh. Shame. But I'll tell you what – put that twenty-pound note in your shoe. By far the safest place for it.'

'Right.'

The man made his way up the steps. 'And, Coco?'

Ricky stopped and looked back. '*What?*'

'You can call me Felix,' the man said. 'One name's as good as another, and maybe we'll meet again.'

In your dreams, Ricky thought as he scrambled up the steps, and away from the weirdo with no hair but many names. *In your dreams.*

* * *

Home, for Ricky, was a single room in a dilapidated house on the outskirts of Hackney. The other occupants of the house changed from week to week, but Ricky had learned not to talk to them anyway. No normal person would stay there. The whole house stank of rotten wood and mildew and there was the scurrying sound of rodents in the ceiling day and night. The room itself contained nothing but a single bed and a sink in the corner with a tap that never stopped dripping. Nobody ever cleaned the toilet that he had to share with several others, and as a result it was too disgusting for words.

It cost Ricky £150 a month to stay there. On the first day of each month, his landlord would arrive to collect the money. Baxter was a frightening man – he had a gaunt face and hardly any lips. Whenever Ricky handed over his money, Baxter would carefully count every last note. He'd never asked Ricky his age, and if it worried him that a kid was living in a dump like this, he didn't show it.

Ricky had seen what happened when someone failed to pay up. Baxter had a couple of heavies who always waited in the car on rent day. If anyone was even fifty p short, the heavies would kick them out of the house. It usually involved some bruises, and occasionally a cut lip.

– *At least we've got another twenty-four hours till*

rent day, Ricky thought as he tramped, footsore, towards the house.

– *Then what's Baxter's Mercedes doing parked in the street?*

Ricky stopped and blinked. The Mercedes was twenty-five metres away, parked right outside the house. There was no doubt that it was Baxter's. A silver Merc stuck out in this part of town.

– *What does he want?*

Ricky walked past the vehicle. It was empty. That meant Baxter's heavies were inside the house. And *that* meant trouble.

There was a commotion inside the house. Something was happening on the first floor, where Ricky's bedroom was. He climbed the stairs nervously. Sure enough, there on the landing were Baxter and two thick-set men – square jaws, flat noses, scars all over their faces. Ricky called them the Chuckle Brothers. Just his little joke. They weren't the type to chuckle.

– *What are the Chuckle Brothers doing outside our room?* Ziggy said.

The heavies were standing on both sides of Ricky's bedroom door, while Baxter loitered a couple of metres from them.

'Ah, there you are, kid,' said Baxter. He had the voice of a thousand cigarettes. 'Been waiting for you.'

'It's rent day tomorrow, not today,' Ricky said. He didn't try to keep the dislike from his voice. His landlord was a scumbag.

'Not for you, kid. You're out of here.'

Ricky stopped at the top of the stairs. 'What do you mean?'

'You stupid as well as ugly?' Baxter said. The Chuckle Brothers gave a nasty laugh, just as a woman appeared in the doorway of Ricky's room. She had three children with her – hungry, pale-faced things. Immediately Ricky understood. Baxter had managed to squeeze more money out of this woman than he could out of Ricky.

'I've got nowhere to go,' Ricky said.

'Anyone bring a violin?' Baxter asked. He nodded at Chuckle 1, who picked up a bag at his feet and threw it towards Ricky. 'Your stuff,' Baxter said. 'And you owe me money.'

'What for?'

'For the damage you've done to the room, you thieving little runt. Peeling wallpaper, cigarette burns—'

'They were there when I moved in – I don't even smoke. And anyway, I haven't got any money.'

'When did *your* problems become *my* problems, kid?' Baxter looked over his shoulder at Chuckle 1. 'Turn out his pockets.'

– You need that money! Run!

But Ricky didn't move. His eyes were on the bag. There wouldn't be much in there. A change of clothes, some toiletries. But it would contain the only two things that *meant* anything to Ricky: a picture in a frame of him with his mum, dad and sister, before the accident. And a letter, rather dog-eared now, in his sister's neat handwriting. He wasn't leaving without them.

The bag was three metres away. Baxter's man was four metres beyond it.

– I can grab it before he gets me, then run down the stairs.

– No you can't. Leave it and get out of here.

But that wasn't an option. Not if the picture was in the bag. Ricky ran forward and grabbed it – it wasn't heavy – then spun round and sprinted back towards the top of the stairs. He was just about to make the first step down when he felt a fist in the small of his back. He lost his balance and tumbled. His shin cracked against the corner of one of the steps and his head hit the banister. He called out in pain as he thumped down the stairs, dragging the bag behind him.

And when he hit the bottom of the stairs, Chuckle 1 was there, behind him. He pulled Ricky to his feet, then thumped him in the pit of his stomach. Winded, Ricky doubled over, but then felt his attacker pull him up by his shoulders. He knew the punch in the face was coming, but didn't expect it to be so hard. Chuckle 1's knuckles connected with his cheek. He felt blood spurt from his nose, and a cracking, pulsing pain on the right side of his face. Chuckle 1 patted him down. He found the money in his back pocket in no time. He waved it up towards Baxter, who was standing at the top of the stairs.

'How much?' Baxter asked.

Chuckle 1 flicked through the wad of notes. 'Hundred and five . . . no, ten . . .' He sounded like he was having trouble with the adding up.

Ricky's winded lungs were still gasping for air, but in the quiet of his mind, Ziggy was feeding him instructions.

– Run now, while he's got his hands full of money. The front door's open – you can feel the air coming in. If you get out of this with just a punch in the stomach, you'll have done well. You've seen what they've done to other people . . .

True enough. These guys thought nothing of breaking a few bones. Ricky gripped the handle of his bag, gulped once more for air and sprinted towards the front door.

Baxter shouted: 'Get him!' But Ricky had found

his legs. Seconds later he had burst out of the front door and was sprinting down the road.

— I seem to have done a lot of running today.

— Well, don't stop now, unless you want another fist in your face.

Ricky's lungs burned. He looked over his shoulder. Twenty metres behind him, Baxter and his men were at the door of the house. Baxter was gesticulating at them, clearly telling them where to run in order to cut Ricky off.

— Remember what that weird man said: 'When you know you're faster than someone, run in a straight line. Otherwise they might out-think you, like I just did.'

Good advice. Ricky kept running to the end of the street, across the main road that ran at right angles to it and straight down another street that continued in the same direction. When he looked back over his shoulder five minutes later, Baxter and his heavies were nowhere to be seen.

He stopped at a children's playground in an area of open parkland alongside the road. It was empty, which was hardly surprising, since the swings were padlocked and out of order, there were graffiti on the play panels and a heap of litter on the ground. Ricky sat at the bottom of the slide and took a moment to catch his breath.

With sweaty hands he opened up the bag and

rooted around inside it for the precious photograph and the letter. They were still there at the bottom. The glass of the photo frame had cracked, but that didn't matter. He could still see the photo of him, his mum and his dad sitting on a park bench, his older sister Madeleine between them. They were all laughing at a long-forgotten joke. And the letter was still snugly tucked inside its envelope.

He carefully put his treasures back into the bag. Then he looked around to check nobody was watching him, before removing his right trainer. Inside, carefully folded up, was the twenty-pound note.

For the second time in the last few minutes, he felt a moment of gratitude for the advice he had received from that odd-bod with the bald head and bad teeth. This was now the only money he had in the world.

– *And you don't even have a place to live.*

– *Shut up. I'll think of something.*

But right now, he couldn't think what that something would be.

3

FEEDING TIME

Even a B & B was out of the question. Too expensive, even if he could nick more money first, and a kid Ricky's age could never book a room without somebody asking questions.

He quickly rejected the idea of approaching the Thrownaways. He didn't need any more fights, or any more scars.

Ricky bitterly resented the loss of his room. Baxter might have been loathsome, but at least he didn't care that Ricky was only fourteen years old.

He needed *somewhere* to sleep. The thought of being alone on the streets, all night, frightened him. Anything could happen there.

At first, he felt like he was wandering aimlessly. But as dusk arrived, he found himself walking footsore along the Euston Road. He realized that he had been heading for central London all along. He felt slightly more comfortable there, at least during the day. The bustle and the noise were the closest he ever got to having company. In any case, all the vagrants seemed to congregate there. And he was one of them now.

– *We have to eat*, Ziggy said.

True. Ricky was weak with hunger. Certainly too weak to pick someone's pocket. You needed your wits about you when you did that, and all he could think about now was his hunger pangs. His stomach groaned as he walked past pizza restaurants and steak houses. As he looked in through the windows, his reflection stared back – his right eye was so swollen it was almost closed up. He touched it gently, then winced. He could forget about pickpocketing for several days. To do that, you needed to be invisible. With a face like this, he was anything but.

He wondered how little of his twenty pounds he could spend in return for a full belly. Eventually he decided chocolate bars were his best bet – cheap and filling – so he bought two Snickers from a Tesco Metro, then started looking for somewhere to settle down and eat them.

He chose Bloomsbury Square. He liked it there among the old university buildings. It had a patch of garden in the middle, with several little thickets of trees dotted around. The garden was surrounded by high railings, and there were benches that he could sit on – and, perhaps later, sleep on. He chose a bench on the north side of the garden, where he sat down to eat. He had to stop himself from wolfing down the chocolate bars, savouring each mouthful slowly. Experience told him that food would be in short supply in the days and weeks to come, so he should enjoy it while he had it.

As he ate, he looked around the gardens. He wasn't alone. On the far side, two women and one man were sipping from cans of lager. They looked to Ricky like they were homeless. You started to recognize the signs after a while – the old clothes, the long hair, the look of hopelessness. A couple of teenage girls were sitting on another bench, chatting and playing music from their phones. A middle-aged man was walking his dog. Ricky kept his head down and concentrated on his food.

– *They're watching you.*

– *I know. I saw them.*

The homeless trio with the lager were staring at him. No doubt they too recognized a fellow vagrant. But Ricky noticed something else in their stare.

– *They've seen you've got food. Food means money. They're thinking, you're just a kid. You should get out of here before they go for you.*

But Ricky was too exhausted to move. He finished his chocolate, but kept half an eye on the trio who were taking so much interest in him.

Five minutes passed. It was fully dark now. Another man entered the gardens. He looked official – blazer, peaked cap. He walked up to the two girls listening to music. Ricky couldn't hear their conversation but he could tell what was happening. They were being asked to leave. He glanced at the big iron gate through which he'd entered the gardens, and realized that it must be locked at night. Clearly nobody wanted homeless people loitering here after dark.

The girls turned off their music and the park-keeper headed over to the dog-walker.

The three down-and-outs, however, still had their eyes on Ricky. They stood up, so Ricky did the same. He didn't really want to leave this square – it would be a good place to stay the night, he had decided, because if he was locked inside he would be protected from the street. But it looked like he needed to get ready to run again.

The dog-walker was making his way towards the gate. Now the park-keeper was approaching the vagrants. He stood in front of them, blocking their view of Ricky.

– *Hide. Now, while nobody's watching. You'll be safe*

locked inside the square for the night, where nobody can get at you . . .

The nearest thicket was about five metres away. Ricky grabbed his bag and stealthily headed towards it. Seconds later, he was hidden among the leaves and low branches. Something scratched his bruised face and he winced, but kept quiet.

A tiny gap in the foliage gave him a view onto the square. The vagrants were walking towards the exit while the park-keeper looked around to check there was nobody else to kick out. He seemed satisfied, but the same couldn't be said of the woman holding her can of lager. She had a scary, raddled, pock-marked face. In his time on the streets, Ricky had learned to recognize the features of a drug addict, and he was looking at them now.

And unlike the park-keeper she seemed to look straight through the foliage at Ricky's exact position.

– *She knows you're here.*

– *Too right.*

'Get a move on!' the park-keeper shouted. The woman swayed slightly, but then she obediently followed the others to – and through – the gate, which the park-keeper locked behind him with a big iron key.

Ricky didn't move. From his hiding place he kept his eyes on the scary woman. Silhouetted in the darkness, she reminded him of a witch in a story book his mum had once read him. The witch was talking to her companions. Ricky held his breath, hoping that they would disappear. But they didn't. They started to circle the garden.

He watched, breathlessly, as the scary woman prowled round the railings. 'I know you're in there, kid,' she hissed when she was just a few metres from Ricky's position. 'You'd better pass us any money you've got, if you don't want us to be waiting for you in the morning.'

– Stay still!

The witch gave a harsh laugh and retreated.

The darkness deepened. The only light came from the vehicles circling Bloomsbury Square. Ricky started to shiver.

– Put some more clothes on.

He pulled a threadbare jumper out of his bag. It helped a bit. He peered towards the railings again. They were about two metres high, with sharp points on the top. Nobody was getting in here tonight. He was safe, until morning.

Ricky lay on the cold ground and used his bag as a pillow. The earth leached the warmth from his body and he started to shiver and ache. His swollen, painful face felt twice its usual size. He tried to sleep, but sleep wouldn't come. He soon grew hungry again, and wished he'd saved one of his chocolate bars.

He sat up and removed the letter from his sister from his rucksack. His hands always trembled slightly when he removed the single piece of paper from the envelope. Before he unfolded it, he sniffed the paper. He sometimes thought he could smell Madeleine's perfume, but maybe that was his mind playing tricks. He opened it up and started to read, only just able to pick out the letters in the gloom:

> Dearest Ricky,
> I know you won't understand what I'm about to do, but you have to believe me when I say it's for the best . . .

Ricky closed his eyes and folded the paper again. He couldn't bear to read on tonight. He tucked the letter carefully back into his rucksack, and tried to sleep again.

The hours passed slowly. In the small hours of the morning he sat up and once more peered through the foliage towards the railings. The traffic had died down now and there were only a few late-night passers-by. He tried to pick out their faces, to see if any of them was the witch. But it was too dark to tell.

– Maybe she's wandered off to find someone else to steal from.

– Yeah. Maybe.

Or maybe not.

Thoughts rebounded in his head as he tried to plan his next move. He couldn't pick pockets with a face like this. Could the remains of his twenty pounds last until his bruises healed? It would have to . . .

Ricky had once heard someone say that the darkest hour came just before dawn. He didn't know if that was true, but it was certainly the coldest. His body had given up shivering, like it didn't have the energy. He was numb and could barely feel his own limbs. He forced himself to stand up in an attempt to get his blood moving.

And that was when he saw them. Three silhouettes.

Like dangerous animals in a zoo, they prowled along the railings on either side of the gate. Occasionally they stopped, held the railings and looked in. From a distance, Ricky recognized the witch's face. It was drawn and lean, and there was a nasty hunger in her eyes – like a predator that knew there was an easy meal within reach. He looked at the other silhouettes in turn. One of them was female, the other male. All thin. All with the same desperate look in their eyes.

— *They've probably got knives. You should hand over your money now. Save yourself getting cut.*

— *No way. That'll leave me with nothing. I'll starve . . .*

— *Maybe I should stash what I've got left in my shoe again . . .*

But he only had coins now, and if he stuffed those in his shoe they would hinder him if he had to run. Not that he thought he'd be able to run, he was so cold. This was going to end ugly.

The grey light of dawn arrived. As the traffic started to build up again, the vultures continued to loiter around the square. And when, an hour after first light, the park-keeper returned to open up the gate, they thronged around it. Feeding time.

The witch was the first to enter, along with one of her companions, a man with tombstone teeth and tattoos over his neck. The others loitered by the gate, obviously ready to catch Ricky if he made a run for it.

— *She's coming your way.*

— *Thanks. I noticed.*

— *What are you going to do?*

Ricky picked up his bag, then stepped out from behind the foliage where he had spent the night. When she saw him, the witch's lip curled. 'Looks like we got ourselves a score,' she rasped nastily to her companion. 'Empty your pockets out, cutie pie. Let's see your money,' she snarled. 'And your shoes. I'll have those trainers too . . .'

Ricky didn't move.

An irritated look flashed across the woman's face. She was wearing a dirty grey tracksuit top, which she unzipped now. From inside, she pulled out a flick-knife, and with the press of a thumb the blade sprang out.

'You heard what I said.'

Ricky stepped back. He couldn't take his eyes off the knife. It looked thin and vicious.

'Cut him,' said the man. 'Just cut him . . .'

– *Over there!*

Ricky's glance shot towards the gate. He blinked. The witch's other accomplice was on the ground, writhing in pain. And just inside the gate, striding towards them with a slight limp, his stick held like a weapon, was a familiar face.

Felix.

And he looked like he meant business.

The witch ran forward. She was just a couple of

metres from Ricky, and he staggered back as she raised her knife in a stabbing motion. He could see her teeth, yellow and crooked, and smell the foulness of her breath. But he could also see Felix, standing right behind her now, his eyes slightly narrowed and a serious look on his strange face. One hand was leaning on his walking stick. In the other he carried a small, white paper bag.

'Would you like a mint humbug?' he said quietly.

The woman froze. She looked over her shoulder. When she saw Felix standing there, with his walking stick and his white paper bag of sweets, she sneered.

'Get out of it, Grandad,' she said, before turning back to Ricky.

Felix's stick moved so fast that Ricky barely saw it. It cracked against the woman's raised wrist and there was a sudden splintering sound as she dropped the knife. She gasped in pain and grabbed her wrist with her good hand while her companion ran towards the gate. Ricky saw from the corner of his eye that the other woman had also got up and run away.

The witch was staggering back, still clutching her wrist. Felix put the bag of sweets in his pocket, then picked up the flick-knife, made it safe, stuck it in his pocket too, and strode up to Ricky. 'It's totally up to you,' he said mildly, 'but I suggest you come with me.'

'You've been following me.' Ricky's voice sounded high-pitched. Tense. Slightly wild.

'Yep. Good job too. Look at the state you're in. She'd have murdered you.' There was sweat on his forehead, even though the morning air was chilly.

'I don't like being followed.'

'I should get used to it, if I were you,' Felix muttered.

'What do you mean?'

Felix stared him straight in the eye. 'I've got two things to say to you, Coco. Will you listen?'

Ricky eyed Felix's walking stick nervously. 'OK,' he said.

'Number one. Staying here was a bad move. You were locked in. *Never* lock yourself in. That means no escape route, and you *always* want an escape route.'

'Right. Thanks for the advice. Very useful.' He darted his eyes left and right. Just to check.

'And number two, you need a hot drink and a hot meal. I'll buy you one now. While you eat, I've got a proposition for you. If you agree to it, great. If not, you'll never see me again. Do we have a deal?'

The only part that Ricky really heard was the bit about the hot meal.

– *Bite his arm off,* said Ziggy. *Get some breakfast inside us, then we can ditch him.*

– *Too right.*

Ricky smiled falsely at Felix. 'All right, mister,' he said. 'Deal.'

4

THE DEAL

'You've got a decision to make,' said Felix.

Ricky stared at his food. Right now, the only decision on his mind was whether to start with the sausage or the bacon. Or the beans – the beans *did* look good. He shovelled a forkful into his mouth, then closed his eyes in bliss as they almost scalded his tongue. After a night on the cold, hard ground of Bloomsbury Square, the warm fug of this café with its steamed-up windows and mugs of hot tea was as welcome as a soft mattress and a cosy duvet.

He cut off a large piece of sausage and crammed it into his mouth. Only then did it twig that Felix had said something. 'What?'

Felix smiled. 'Finish your food,' he said. 'Then we'll talk.' He sat back in his chair and let his eyes wander, sucking on one of his mint humbugs and humming softly to himself as Ricky tucked in. This guy truly was a weirdo, but he was a weirdo with a wallet, and for Ricky, being full had never felt so good. As he scraped the last remains of bacon fat and ketchup from his plate with the edge of his fork, he saw that Felix was looking at him with that amused expression he so often seemed to wear.

'What?' Ricky said.

'It saves on washing up, I suppose.'

Ricky lowered his knife and fork. 'Thanks for the food,' he said. His eyes flickered towards the door.

— *You could just leave now.*

— *No, look, it's raining outside. Hear baldy out. Then we'll go.*

'So, Coco . . .'

'My name's not Coco.'

'I know. It's Ricky.'

Ricky stared at him, horrified. *He has to be some kind of official,* he thought wildly.

— *Has he come to drag you back to the do-gooders?*

'How did you know that?' he stammered at last.

'I know lots of things.'

'Like what?'

'Like, that landlord of yours is in for an extremely bad day. Baxter, isn't it? He got a knock on the door about two hours ago. He'll be in police custody by now.'

'What about his tenants?'

'You should be pleased,' Felix said. 'Baxter is a very unpleasant individual. Look what he did to your face.'

'It's not as easy as that. His tenants will have nowhere to go. It's complicated.'

'Complicated?' Felix said, amusement dancing in his eyes. 'Yes it is, Coco. I'm glad you understand that. Sometimes we all have to do complicated things.'

'Stop calling me Coco!' There was a pause. Ricky gave Felix a hard stare. '*Have* you been following me?'

'Yes.'

'I didn't see you.'

'I'm very good at it.'

'How do you know my name?'

'The same way I know that your mum and dad died in a car crash thanks to a drunk driver on the M25 on the third of February last year. The same way I know that your sister Madeleine committed suicide soon afterwards . . .'

Ricky looked away. There were some things he couldn't bear to hear spoken out loud.

There was a pause. When Felix continued, his voice was slightly more kindly. 'The same way I know that you ran away from your foster parents in Northampton because they wanted you to be a member of their church. All a bit happy-clappy for someone who'd just lost his mum and dad. And his sister, of course.'

Ricky's eyes narrowed. Maybe that was it. Maybe this guy wasn't a criminal after all, but had been sent to find Ricky and drag him back into care.

'I'm *not* going back to the do-gooders, if that's your plan,' Ricky said. 'And *definitely* not to that bunch of weirdo God-botherers again. I'd rather live on the street.' He glanced at the door again. If he moved quickly, he could get away.

Felix inclined his head. 'Maybe we can sort things so you don't have to do either.'

– *The rain's easing off*, Ziggy said. *We can go now.*

But Ricky wasn't ready to go. He wanted to know more.

'I'm impressed by you,' Felix was saying. 'I like the way you work alone, not like those other kids in Trafalgar Square. And you're quite skilful . . .'

'But *you* caught me,' Ricky pointed out.

Another smile. 'Of course, Coco. *I'd* catch any-one.' Another gentle smile. 'I know, I know, it seems unlikely, doesn't it? Still, I can tell that you're a fast learner, and you've certainly got some guts. Most runaways would have crumbled by now, but you've got a bit of steel. That goes a long way, in certain lines of work.'

Ricky's eyes narrowed. 'What are you, some sort of Fagin?'

'Ah, so you're well-read too,' Felix said, avoiding the question.

Ricky wasn't, but he'd watched the musical of *Oliver!* with his sister once, and with a pang he remembered them both singing along to the 'pick a pocket or two' song. At the time, of course, he had had no idea that he would himself end up as a pickpocket. A modern Artful Dodger.

– But without a Fagin to take your profits, Ziggy reminded him.

'I like that. You can learn a lot from books,' Felix continued. He slid his hand into the inside pocket of his jacket and pulled out a piece of A4 paper, which he handed to Ricky. 'Have a look,' he said.

It looked like an estate agent's particulars for an apartment. A very cool top-floor apartment. It overlooked the river, had large rooms and state-of-the-art fittings. Ricky laid the paper on the table. 'I think the rent might be a bit high for a pickpocket's wages,' he said.

'There won't be any rent,' said Felix. 'That's your new pad, if you want it to be.'

Alarm bells.

– He's one of those blokes they always warned you about. Get out of here, quick.

'Believe me, I know what you're thinking,' Felix said quietly. He removed the knife he had confiscated from the woman in Bloomsbury Square, and slid it across the table. 'Take that,' he said. 'If I or anyone else tries something you don't like, you can defend yourself.'

Ricky took the knife, but shuddered as he gripped it – he hated blades.

'You're probably wondering why I just came down with a bad case of generosity,' said Felix.

'What I'm wondering,' said Ricky, 'is where's the catch.'

Felix did not, Ricky noticed, deny that there was one. He just continued talking as if Rick hadn't spoken.

'Here's the deal. You move into this flat. You get a hundred pounds a week spending money. You stop with the pickpocketing and the thievery. You eat properly, you sleep properly and you spend your spare time taking lessons.'

– Lessons?

'What are you, some sort of, I dunno, top-secret geography teacher? I'm not going back to school, you know.'

'We're not talking school, Coco. And we're certainly not talking geography.'

– *So what is he talking?*

– *Think about it. He's already taught you stuff. Useful stuff. The twenty-pound note, the running in a straight line, the escape route.*

– *But why? What does he want from us?*

– *Maybe he is some sort of Fagin. Training up kids to carry out his crimes for him.*

– *So what do we do?*

'There's no pressure,' Felix said. 'You do what you want. The choice is yours.' He sat back in his seat again, as though he'd said his piece.

'What if I say no?'

Felix gave a little shrug. 'There's always Blooms-bury Square, and plenty of other places like it. But I've got to tell you, Coco, it didn't look all *that* comfortable. Then again, there's the – "do-gooders", did you call them? The child-protection people will catch up with you, I expect.'

'No *way*. I'm *not* going back. I'll hide . . .'

'And they'll find you, Coco. They'll definitely find you, eventually.'

They stared at each other across the table. Ricky had the distinct impression that he was be-ing outmanoeuvred. He picked up the piece of paper with the photos again. It looked a lot nicer than

Baxter's horrible rented accommodation.

But what was he getting himself into?

– *Here's what we do. We rest up in this flat of his. We take his money. We learn what we can, if that's so important to him. We definitely find out how he's following us. Then we disappear again.*

As these thoughts went through his mind, Ricky shifted uncomfortably in his seat. Felix was giving him a piercing stare. It felt like he knew exactly what Ricky was thinking.

'OK,' Ricky said quietly.

Felix nodded, his brow furrowed. He took out a ten-pound note and laid it on the table to pay for Ricky's breakfast. 'Shall we go?' he said.

The rain had stopped, but the pavements were still glistening. Felix hailed a cab by holding out his sturdy walking stick. He gave the driver an instruction as Ricky climbed inside the taxi. Moments later, they were being whisked down High Holborn and towards the City.

'Where are we headed?' Ricky asked.

'Docklands. It's a penthouse flat. Big building, lots of glass. I think you'll like it.'

Ricky didn't reply.

'It's certainly better than a park bench, anyway,' said Felix.

* * *

Three hundred and fifty miles to the north-west of London, three men stood on a hill overlooking a bleak, grey sea. There was a stiff breeze which ruffled their hair and their expensive suits. To their west, shrouded in mist, they could just see the outline of an industrial shipyard, perhaps five miles away. Behind them, on the brow of the hill, an official-looking black Mercedes was waiting. But the attention of these three men was all on the open water.

Two of them were broad-shouldered. The third was rather wiry with a mean, pinched face. He had a pair of binoculars, and he was looking intently through them, out to sea. The broad-shouldered men looked annoyed at having to stand in the long, wet grass. It was soaking their good leather shoes and the bottoms of their trousers.

'What is this, Cole?' one of them said. He had a very pronounced Russian accent. That, and the howling wind, meant that the wiry man struggled to understand him. 'Some sort of joke?'

Cole did not lower his binoculars. 'No joke, Dmitri,' he said. 'Just keep watching.'

The two broad-shouldered men frowned and looked out to sea. It was rough and uninviting.

'I don't even know where we are,' said the second burly man. 'Why have you brought us to this horrible place?'

Cole finally lowered his binoculars. With a great deal of obvious effort, he gave the man a thin smile.

'It's the Firth of Clyde, Gregoriev. I admit it's not quite as lovely as your Siberian coastline.' The men frowned at his little dig. Cole raised the binoculars again, and once more looked out to sea. 'You'll understand why we're here soon enough. Just give it a few more minutes.'

'It has been half an hour already.' Gregoriev sounded aggressive. Cole glanced in his direction and saw his right hand head towards his coat pocket. At the last moment, Dmitri grabbed his wrist and said something in Russian. Gregoriev lowered his hand, but didn't sound any less annoyed when he said: 'I think you're pretending to know something you—'

'*Quiet!*' Cole instructed.

The men were silent. The wind howled around them. Ten seconds later, Cole said: 'There!'

The two Russians squinted and peered out to sea. 'What?' Dmitri said. 'Where?'

But Cole was the only one who could see, through the powerful magnification of the binoculars. About half a mile out to sea, something had just broken through the surface. It looked, at first, like the hump of a whale, but darker. Water sluiced from its rounded top as it emerged from the sea, getting bigger with every second.

But this was just the conning tower of the submarine. A few seconds later, the main body of the sub started to emerge. Black and threatening, it dwarfed the tower and churned up the already rough sea around it.

Cole handed the binoculars to Dmitri, who grabbed them greedily and looked out to sea. 'I still cannot see anything!' he announced immediately. 'What is wrong with these stupid things? I can't s—' He cut himself off short. Clearly he had located the object. He stared at it for a full minute, before passing the binoculars to Gregoriev.

'Vanguard class nuclear submarine,' Cole said as the second Russian continued to look. 'One of four. Fully equipped with Trident II D-5 ballistic missiles.' He waited for Gregoriev to lower his binoculars, then gave the two Russians another of his thin smiles. 'You see, gentlemen, I can show you how to locate any British nuclear submarine, anywhere in the world. Which is valuable information, of course. So shall we talk money?'

The two Russians grinned at each other. 'Not here,' said Dmitri. 'Let us return to the car. There is a helicopter waiting to take us back to London. As we travel, we will be happy to discuss how rich we are going to make you, Mr Cole.'

Without another word, the three men turned

their back on the ocean and walked up the hill to the waiting car.

Felix was right. Ricky *did* like his new home. How could you not?

There was a vast bedroom overlooking the Thames with a huge double bed and a big TV on the wall. The kitchen glistened with quartz and steel and there was a fridge packed full of food and soft drinks. The bathroom had a jacuzzi and a shower with four separate jets. There was a video entryphone, a state-of-the-art computer and a fully equipped gym in a room all by itself.

 – *This is awesome! And free!*

 – *Nothing's for free, buddy. Nothing's for free.*

'Make yourself at home,' Felix said as Ricky stood in the main room, clutching his rucksack, his eyes wide, not quite sure where to look.

'This isn't a wind-up?' he asked.

'Nope. I'll leave you to get settled in. I'll be back tomorrow morning, nine a.m.'

'What for?'

'I told you. Lessons.'

Felix turned his back on Ricky and limped towards the exit.

'Hey, Felix.'

The strange man stopped and turned.

'What happened to your leg?'

Felix's face twitched. It was clearly a painful memory.

'Somebody shot me. The bullet shattered the bones in my lower leg. They had to amputate.'

'Sounds painful.'

'I was lucky they could do it below the knee and not above it. It's a good deal harder to walk without a knee joint. Or so I'm told.'

Ricky thought about that for a moment. 'Does this sort of thing happen often, in your line of work?'

'Amputations?'

'Bullets.'

Felix scratched his nose. 'We try to avoid it.'

'Who's "we"?'

Felix gave him a blank smile. 'It's complicated,' he said calmly. 'Now then, I almost forgot. You'll be needing a key to get in and out.'

'Who's "we"?' Ricky repeated. 'The good guys or the bad guys? *That's* not too complicated for you, is it?'

'I'm surprised you care – it's not like you really intend to stick around long enough to find out.'

Ricky said nothing, but he felt himself blushing.

'Am I right?'

Silence.

'*Am I right?*'

Silence.

'Good,' Felix said, almost as though he was talking to himself. 'Maybe we've learned something already. Now, about that key.'

'Yeah,' Ricky said. 'About that key.'

'It's in the flat somewhere. Your homework is to find it.'

'*What?*'

'Find it, Coco. Use your eyes. Show me how good you are at looking.'

– *He's crazy.*

– *You've only just worked that out?*

Felix was limping towards the exit.

'Hey, Felix?'

'Yes, kid?'

'Who are you, really?'

A pause. Felix put one hand in his pocket and pulled out a mint humbug, which he popped into his mouth.

'Why don't you just think of me as your guardian angel,' he said.

5

HOMEWORK

Friday, 2:30 p.m.

The key was nowhere. Ricky was sure of it. He'd looked through the drawers in the kitchen, inside all the cupboards and even in the fridge. He'd checked under the mattress of his bed and inside all the wardrobes. He'd checked under the rugs in the living room and hallways. He had even found himself on his hands and knees checking behind the U-bend of the toilet, before returning to the kitchen and double-checking the drawers he'd already searched.

It was at that point that he'd decided this was insane. Felix was playing silly games with him. Well, maybe Ricky didn't want to play.

He helped himself to a Coke from the fridge and sat on the balcony overlooking the Thames. It was late afternoon, and he couldn't help thinking about how his life had changed in the past twenty-four hours. He had everything he didn't have yesterday – a place to stay, and food to eat.

But he still felt very uneasy.

Who was this Felix character? Why was he going out of his way to help him? Ricky knew enough about the world to realize that nobody helped anyone unless there was something in it for them.

The sun started to set and the air grew chill. Ricky headed back inside and made himself an enormous chicken and mayonnaise sandwich from the plentiful stores in the kitchen. He walked around the flat as he ate it. He stared at the front door and it occurred to him that, without a key, he was as good as imprisoned in here.

But the key was nowhere.

Ricky felt a little surge of anger towards Felix for setting him an impossible task.

– *I'm trapped. If I leave this flat I'll never get back in again.*

– *But you can leave if you want to. Let's face it though, being stuck here is better than being stuck in Bloomsbury Square.*

He took his holdall into the bedroom. Sitting on the edge of the bed, he pulled out the framed picture of his mum, dad and Madeleine. He stared at it. As often happened, he found himself remembering the moment he heard the news that they had died: the two policemen at the door, Madeleine burying her face in her hands, the way he had sat on the sofa, staring into space, unable to take it all in . . .

Then he snapped out of it and placed the picture on the bedside table. He turned on the TV, lay on the bed and started channel hopping.

There was nothing much on. He spent a couple of minutes watching two kids his own age rapping on *Britain's Got Talent*. He caught the last five minutes of *The Simpsons*. Then he found himself on a news channel. A journalist was standing outside the Russian Embassy in London. He had a serious face and a serious tone. 'Tensions between Russia and the West are mounting over the situation in the Middle East. Talks between the British Foreign Secretary and his Russian counterpart have been described as . . .'

But Ricky never found out how these talks were described. The bed was soft. The room was warm. He had already drifted off into a deep sleep . . .

It was five miles, as the crow flies, from the elegant apartment in which Ricky now slept to an even more elegant mansion, grandly named the White House, in the heart of Mayfair. A human, however, would have to struggle for a couple of hours through the rush-hour crowds to get there.

If they did this – and if they managed to get over the high railings that surrounded the White House and past the security cameras that covered the entrance, they might find themselves climbing an impressive, winding marble staircase and entering a bedroom at the top of the stairs. Here they would find a fifteen-year-old girl called Izzy Cole sitting on the edge of her bed, crying.

The palms of her hands, which covered her face, were soaked in tears. Her shoulders shook. She was *trying* not to cry, she really was. But even when she managed to stop for fifteen or twenty seconds, the tears always returned when she remembered what had just happened.

She had argued with her father about an earring. Such a small thing – a tiny gold stud that lay on Izzy's bedside table. When he had returned home just half an hour ago – looking unusually windswept – he had seemed to be in a rare good mood. So good that Izzy had dared to appear in front of him wearing the earring.

Bad move.

When her father saw it, his mood had changed immediately. He knew that Izzy had defied his instruction that she would never – *never* – have her ears pierced while she lived under his roof. She was the only one of her friends who didn't have pierced ears, of course, but even so. It had seemed like such a small thing to ask the lady in the tattoo parlour to do, especially as her two friends Becky and Caitlin had pretended to be eighteen and were getting actual tattoos – identical roses – on their shoulders.

Her father thought differently.

She hated him. *Hated* him. She knew it made her sound spoiled. She knew she lived in a posh house and went to a posh school and never really went without anything. But it was all a lie. She hated seeing her father on TV, smiling for the cameras – the Right Honourable Jacob Cole, MP, who always sounded so reasonable and who was so popular with *everyone*.

But they didn't know what he was really like. They didn't see the real him.

Izzy took a tissue from the box by her bed. She blew her nose, then winced. She lowered the tissue and looked at it. Blood. She walked across the room to her dressing table, where she looked at her face in the mirror.

Even Izzy was surprised by what she saw. There was a cut on her upper lip where her dad had hit her. The left eye was swollen with a fat purple bruise. She stared in the mirror for a full minute before the cut started to ooze again and she had to grab another tissue to mop it up.

When the bleeding finally stopped she moved over to the window and looked outside. Her room overlooked the front garden. There was a high wall between the garden and the street itself, but from the first floor she could see the opposite pavement. There was an elegant street lamp there, bathing the pavement in the yellow glow of its light. And leaning against the lamp post itself, a figure. He was broad-shouldered, with a heavy overcoat, a bald head with black skin. In one hand he carried a walking stick. Izzy stared at him.

Suddenly he looked up. Izzy felt a chill as their eyes met. The man quickly averted his gaze, then looked down at the pavement and started to walk away. Izzy noticed that he had a slight limp . . .

A moment later he was out of sight. Izzy forgot about him just as quickly. Rebellious thoughts went through her head. She would tell someone about her dad. Make everyone realize what he was really like. This wasn't the first time he'd hit her, she would explain. He was brutal, and violent, and . . .

Her moment of courage quickly vanished. Tell *everyone*? She couldn't even tell her mum, who always took her dad's side because she was even more scared of him than Izzy was. Nobody would ever believe a silly fifteen-year-old girl against the important Jacob Cole, MP. She'd be laughed at, and accused of lying.

All she could do was clean herself up as best she could. Think up some story to explain away the marks on her face. And stay in her bedroom in case the sight of her made her dad even angrier.

It was a nice bedroom. Tastefully decorated with comfortable furniture. But to Izzy, it sometimes felt like a prison.

Ricky awoke suddenly. A harsh-sounding doorbell was buzzing repeatedly, and the morning sun was streaming through the windows. He looked at his watch: 9:06 a.m. Saturday morning. He'd slept right through.

The doorbell buzzed for perhaps the sixth or seventh time.

'Bet it's Felix,' Ricky said under his breath. He jumped off the bed, hurried to the door and, with a quick yank, pulled it open. Felix was there, his usual white paper bag of sweets in his hand and a rucksack over his shoulder.

'Jelly baby?' Felix offered, holding out the bag.

'Er, bit early, actually.'

'Rubbish. It's never too early for a jelly baby. Especially the blackcurrant ones.' He selected a purple jelly baby and popped it in his mouth. 'Have you found it?' he asked.

Ricky blinked. His head was stuffy, his mouth dry. His clothes were rumpled and none too fresh. He shook his head to shake off the sleepiness. 'Found what?' he asked stubbornly.

Felix smiled, then stepped over the threshold as though he owned the place.

– *Maybe he* does *own the place.*

– *He must be very rich if he does.*

Felix was a metre past the door when he stopped as if he'd hit an invisible brick wall. He screwed his face up.

'What's the matter?' Ricky asked.

'You,' he said.

Ricky looked himself up and down. 'What about me?'

'You stink, Coco,' Felix said. 'Like something that's just died. Would you care to clean yourself up before we start?'

'Please, don't hold back,' Ricky said. He felt himself blushing. He supposed Felix was right – he hadn't washed for forty-eight hours, and twelve of those had been spent sleeping rough – but he didn't like being spoken to like that. 'Anyway,' he said, 'I'm fine.'

Felix shrugged, wrinkled his nose and walked further into the apartment.

'So, I *couldn't* find the key,' Ricky said. 'You sure you left me one?'

'Yep,' said Felix, looking over his shoulder as they walked into the front room. 'Where d'you look?'

'Everywhere.'

'Rubbish,' said Felix, dropping his rucksack on the floor. 'If you'd looked *everywhere*, you'd have found it.'

'Well, OK, but nobody can look absolutely *every-where* . . .' Ricky walked towards the kitchen.

'Course they can. They just need to know how. Want me to tell you?'

'Er . . .'

'I'll take that as a yes,' said Felix. 'If you're not going to have a shower, stick the kettle on and make me a brew. Have one yourself, if you like, but my need is greater – I'm going to be doing a lot of talking and you'll be doing a lot of listening. Lessons start now, Coco. Put your brain into gear and get ready to learn.'

Five minutes later they were sitting in the front room, cups of steaming tea in their hands.

'So when you were looking for the key, you just searched in random places, right?' Felix said. 'You thought about *where* it might be, looked in that place, then moved on to another place that popped into your head.'

Ricky peered at him. 'Have you been spying on me again?' he said.

'Not at all. You just did what most people do. You searched without any kind of method. But that's not really searching at all. That's just looking around.'

Ricky opened his mouth, wanting to argue. But then he remembered himself opening random cupboards in the kitchen and realized that Felix was right.

'Maybe you've got a point,' he said.

'How kind of you to say so.' Felix looked around the room. 'So why not try this. When you search a room, divide it up into smaller cubes – in your head, I mean. Search each cube thoroughly before moving on to the next.'

Ricky frowned. 'But some of the cubes will just be empty space,' he said.

'Then they won't take you long to search.' Felix drained his tea and stood up, wincing as he put pressure on his bad leg. 'Here endeth the first lesson,' he said. 'Now find that key.'

'You could just tell me where it is,' Ricky said. He was feeling rather grumpy about the whole key thing.

'Of course I could. But where would be the fun in that? Now find it.'

'What are *you* going to do?'

'If it's all the same to you,' Felix said, 'I think I might have another cup of tea, and perhaps just one more jelly baby.'

As Felix limped off to the kitchen, Ricky stood up. He looked to one end of the room. 'This is stupid,' he muttered. But in his mind, he divided that end of the room into invisible cubes. One of the cubes contained a low wooden dresser, which he searched thoroughly – even going so far as to remove the drawers and check their undersides. Another cube contained a picture on the wall, which he removed to check the back. No key. He looked over his shoulder to see Felix standing in the doorway, watching him intently with a second mug of tea in his hand.

– *This is a waste of your time.*

– *So what? If it keeps him happy, and means we get to stay here . . .*

Ricky smiled at Felix, and went back to his searching.

He found the key ten minutes later. It was stuck with a piece of Blu-tac to the pelmet that covered the curtain rail. Ricky was surprised to feel a little surge of triumph as he held it up. 'One key!' he announced.

'Well done,' said Felix.

'You don't look all that impressed.'

For the first time since they'd met, Ricky saw a flash of irritation cross Felix's face. 'What did you want, Coco? A street parade?'

Ricky felt himself blushing.

'I certainly hope you didn't think that was tough, young man, because you've hardly even started. By the time I've finished with you, you'll be—'

'The best-trained little sneak thief on the streets of London?' Ricky filled in. 'Because that's what you want me for, isn't it? Nobody looks at a kid, nobody suspects a kid. So you need a kid to do your dirty work for you, stealing and stuff. Am I right?'

Felix's face gave nothing away. 'It's complicated,' he said.

Ricky felt a surge of irrational anger at having his phrase thrown back in his teeth again.

'Of course,' Felix continued, 'keys are rather limited in their application.'

'Eh?'

'What I mean is, generally speaking, one key will only open one door. It would be much more useful, don't you think, if we had a key that would open *any* door.'

'I guess.'

Felix smiled. He looked around the room for his rucksack and rummaged inside it, then withdrew what looked like a large staple gun, with a long, narrow blade protruding from one end.

'What's that?' Ricky asked.

'That,' said Felix, 'is a snap gun. Unbelievably useful. Think of it as a gift, if you like.' He threw the snap gun across the room to Ricky – who caught it just in time. 'I've got something else in here for you,' Felix added as he looked inside his rucksack again, before pulling out a solid mortise lock. 'You can practise on this if you like. You just insert the snap gun into the lock, then start squeezing the handle until you get a fit. You'll soon get the hang of it.' He flung the mortise lock across the room as well.

Ricky caught it with his free hand, but winced as it bent his fingers back. Felix, though, already had his attention on something else. He felt into the inside of his jacket pocket and withdrew a book – a paperback, rather dog-eared. He spun it across the room to Ricky, who had to catch it in the crook of his arms because his hands were full.

'You like reading,' Felix said. 'So read.'

Ricky didn't even look at the cover. He just let the book fall onto the coffee table, then laid the snap gun and mortise lock down next to it. 'What good are books to a thief?' he said.

Felix gave him a serious kind of look. Then he limped over to join Ricky on the far side of the room by the window. He pointed out towards London. 'See that,' he said.

'What?'

'Canary Wharf. The City of London. And beyond that, the Houses of Parliament. There are just as many thieves in those places as there are in any prison. Which ones do you think have read more books? The ones in power, or the ones in jail?'

Ricky was silent.

'Read the book, Coco,' Felix said as he stumped back towards the exit. 'And stop calling yourself a thief.'

'Why?' Ricky said. 'It's what I am, isn't it?'

'Oh, you never know,' Felix said, passing one hand over his bald head. 'One day you might surprise yourself.'

He left the room. Ricky stood by the window and listened to the sound of his strange new acquaintance letting himself out of the flat.

6

KIM'S GAME

As Ricky stood in the shower, watching the dirty water sluice down the plughole, he had to admit that Felix might have been right. He *was* filthy. He doused himself in shampoo and soap and came out feeling cleaner than he had done in months.

In the bedroom he found that the clothes hanging in the wardrobe and folded in the drawers fitted him perfectly. He chose a pair of jeans, a Hollister top and some brand-new Nikes, and tried not to think too hard about who had put these clothes here and how they knew his exact size. When he looked at himself in the mirror, he had to inhale sharply. Sure, his hair was still shoulder-length and straggly, but he suddenly looked more like the kid he'd been a year ago: the ordinary kid, with a mum, a dad, a sister and a home to call his own.

He felt that pang of solitude and sorrow that always wormed its way to the surface when he thought about his family. But he quickly buried it again. He was on his own now, and he couldn't afford to start feeling sorry for himself.

He stepped back into the main room. Felix's book was still lying face down on the coffee table.

— *Are we going to read it?*

— *Have you got anything better to do?*

The answer was no. Ricky picked up the book and read the title. *Kim*, by Rudyard Kipling. The pages were yellowed and had the musty smell of old libraries. Ricky liked that smell. He nestled down on the sofa and started to read.

For several hours, he was lost in the book. The story unfolded of an orphaned kid on the streets of India, a strange tale of adventure and mystery. Ricky was transfixed as Kim came under the influence of the British Secret Service, and his eyes were glued to the page as a jewel merchant — himself a Secret Service operative — started training Kim in the techniques of spycraft.

Spycraft.

By the time he turned the last page, it was dark outside. Ricky's eyes lingered on the final paragraph. As he regretfully closed the book, he also closed his eyes.

– Is the book some sort of message? Is that what he's trying to do, turn me into some sort of . . .

Ricky couldn't bring himself to say the word 'spy'. It just sounded too ridiculous. And yet here he was, plucked from the streets and surrounded by—

'Good book?'

Ricky started. Across the gloomy room he saw Felix standing in the doorway.

'I didn't hear you come in,' Ricky accused.

'No,' said Felix. 'It's something I'm very—'

'Yeah, yeah, don't tell me, it's something you're very good at.' For some reason Ricky felt incredibly angry. Like he'd been duped. Felix hadn't mentioned anything about spying. Now Ricky felt like he was just playing stupid, *stupid* games. 'What is it this evening? Wine gums?'

'God, no. Can't stand them. But if you'd like a cola bottle—'

'I'm going out,' Ricky shouted.

He stormed past Felix, who watched him without expression, slamming the front door of the flat as he left. The lift on the other side of the corridor was waiting for him, and it moved maddeningly slowly as it carried him down to the ground floor. Here a concierge sitting behind the large marble reception desk nodded politely. Ricky felt the concierge's eyes follow him as he crossed the entrance hall, and he felt a moment of paranoia. But when he looked back over his shoulder, the concierge was simply reading a magazine.

It was humid outside. The apartment block faced out onto a large pedestrian square with small, neatly trimmed trees spaced symmetrically, and benches around the edges. Only a few of the benches were occupied. A couple kissing at the far end. A tramp, fiercely clutching a can of beer. Next to him were two youths, a boy and a girl, their faces covered with piercings. They were Thrownaways, Ricky could tell at a glance. He kept his distance, but found himself wondering where *they* would be sleeping tonight.

The thought stopped him in his tracks. He looked back up at the apartment block behind him.

– Where will you *be sleeping, Ricky, if we just walk away now?*

His eyes crept up to the top floor. He wondered if Felix was at the window, looking out.

– If you walk away now, what are your chances of coming back? You've got an opportunity, Ricky. It won't last for ever, but while it does you should milk it for all it's worth. Smile sweetly at the guy. Listen to everything he has to say. You can do a runner any time you like.

'Just not tonight,' Ricky muttered out loud. He did an about turn and walked back into the apartment block lobby. This time, the concierge's eyes really did follow him all the way to the lift.

Back on the top floor, he let himself into the flat with the key he'd had such trouble finding. Felix was still there, looking out of the window as Ricky had imagined him. He turned and raised one eyebrow.

'Sorry,' said Ricky. He did his best to look like he meant it. Like he hadn't just returned because he didn't have anywhere else to go. 'Got a bit freaked out.'

'Don't apologize, Coco. You can leave whenever you want.'

'I . . . I don't want to.'

'Glad to hear it.' Felix held up a pack of playing cards. 'Let's play Kim's game.'

Ricky blinked at him. 'What do you mean?'

'I thought you said you'd read the book.'

'I have.'

'So you'll remember the jewel game.'

Ricky nodded. Now he thought about it, he *did* remember it. In the book, a servant had shown Kim a tray full of jewels. When the tray was covered up, Kim had to describe what jewels were there. The agent had practised it over and over, with different objects, until he was able to memorize almost anything at a single glance.

'Can't stretch to jewels, I'm afraid,' Felix added. 'We'll use playing cards. That's how I learned it in the army. All special forces practise this till they're blue in the face.'

They sat opposite each other on either side of the coffee table. Felix laid out ten cards and gave Ricky twenty seconds to memorize them. He got seven right.

'Not bad, for a first time,' Felix said. But Ricky could tell by the way he looked at him that he was more impressed than he wanted to let on. 'Now try again. I'll shuffle the pack.'

It took eight goes before Ricky could memorize all ten cards. Felix reduced the time he was allowed to look at them to fifteen seconds. Then ten. It was tiring work but when, after an hour, Felix called a halt, Ricky was strangely disappointed. He was in the zone and wanted to continue.

'It's getting late, Coco,' Felix said. 'You need your beauty sleep.' He frowned. 'No offence intended.'

Ricky ignored that comment. He watched Felix collect the cards and stack them neatly on the coffee table.

'That thing you mentioned,' he said. 'About learning this game in the army.'

'What about it?'

'Is that where you lost your leg? In the army?'

Felix sniffed. He looked as though he was deciding whether or not to answer. 'Yeah,' he said finally.

'What happened?'

'I already told you. A bullet.'

'Yeah, but . . . how?'

'I was an intelligence officer. And I made a mistake. A very bad mistake.' He gave Ricky a piercing look. 'It's always your mistakes that get you. Remember that.'

'What was yours?'

'I used a torch.'

Ricky blinked, not understanding, so Felix continued.

'I went undercover into an enemy-held village. It was night time. I needed to search an empty house and I used my torch to help me see. Trouble is, if someone's watching, a torch is the worst thing to use at night. When people see a light moving around inside a house, it always raises their suspicions. The best thing to do is switch a lamp on. Nobody bats an eyelid about that. But there was no lamp inside the house, and I didn't have night-vision goggles . . .'

His voice trailed away for a moment as Ricky sat in stunned silence.

'Anyway,' Felix said suddenly, 'an enemy

sympathizer saw me leaving from a distance. He waited until he thought I was clear of the village, then he took a pot shot and got lucky.'

'What sort of gun was it?'

'Does it matter?' Felix said. His voice was unusually forceful.

'Sorry,' Ricky said quickly. He felt he'd overstepped the mark. This wasn't something Felix liked to discuss.

They stood in awkward silence for a moment, before Felix said: 'A 7.62 Nato round from a bolt-action M24 sniper rifle.'

'I'm sorry,' Ricky said again.

'Don't be. I was one of the lucky ones. A few centimetres higher and I'd have been killed.'

Ricky absorbed that information for a moment. 'Is that what you are, then?' he said. 'An intelligence officer?'

'What I am,' said Felix, 'is very tired. It's nearly ten o'clock. I need to get some sleep, and so do you. I'll see you first thing in the morning.'

And without another word he left the flat.

As Felix walked out of that luxury apartment in the Docklands, a much younger man sprinted down a flight of stone steps into the basement of a derelict building in a dark, forgotten side street of Soho. He was sweating, out of breath and frightened.

The building was called Keeper's House. It had been condemned for years. Its windows were boarded up, its walls covered in graffiti, and lengths of guttering hung limply from the roof. Inside, it smelled of wet rot and neglect. The rooms on the ground floor were littered with old furniture – mouldy, ripped sofas, tables riddled with wood-worm. Anything remotely usable had been moved down to the basement.

The young man's name was Tommy. He was sixteen years old, with scruffy black hair and a pro-nounced Adam's apple. He wore a permanent scowl and always seemed to have cuts on his knuckles or face – the result of some fight or other. He had a lot of fights on the street.

He burst into the main basement room.

'Thought you'd forgotten about us,' rasped a voice. Tommy looked over to see a figure, slightly smaller than him, hunched over in the corner of the room. It was too gloomy to make out his features very clearly, but Tommy recognized Hunter's voice well enough.

'Would I do that?' Tommy replied sarcastically.

He peered around the large basement room. It was lit by an old standard lamp in the corner – somehow, Hunter had managed to rig up some electricity – and contained a mismatched collection of furniture and people.

The furniture was old. The people were all young. Tommy was easily the eldest, and one of the kids, who was sitting in the corner hugging his knees, couldn't be more than twelve, though he swore blind he was fifteen. There were eight of them in the room, including Tommy and Hunter. The others were either still out on the street or in one of the other basement rooms that adjoined this one.

Tommy looked anxiously over his shoulder, then back towards Hunter.

There was a moment of silence. Then Hunter moved from the shadows into the centre of the room. His features became visible. Hunter was in his sixties, with a square jaw and a nose that had been broken several times. He had a sharp, violent face and watery, greedy eyes.

'What's the matter with you?' he demanded.

Tommy closed his eyes. 'Police,' he breathed.

A nasty pause as Hunter stared at him. 'Did they follow you?'

'I think I lost them.'

Another silence. Tommy felt the eyes of all the other kids in the room burning into him.

'You *think* you lost them?'

'Y . . . yeah . . .'

'Well,' Hunter said in a dangerous half-whisper, 'that's all right then, isn't it? He *thinks* he lost them. You got anything for me?'

Tommy swallowed hard, then nodded. He stepped further into the room and held out a fat black wallet. Hunter snatched it and started rifling through its contents. He clearly wasn't interested in the credit cards – they were too easy to trace. But he fished out several notes and a handful of change which he shoved in his pocket before discarding the wallet. 'That the best you can do?' he said. 'On a Saturday night?'

Tommy nodded.

'And I suppose you want something to eat? Go on then, son. It's over there.'

Tommy had already noticed the pizza boxes on a table against the right-hand wall. There were five, all open. He walked up to the table to see that only one of the boxes had any food left in it – two slices of cold, congealed pizza. He knew not to complain. Instead, he grabbed a slice and started cramming it hungrily into his mouth.

The blow, when it came, knocked all the wind from his lungs and half the food from his mouth. He collapsed, barely able to breathe, and saw Hunter standing over him, still carrying the short, stout cudgel he'd just used to whack him in the stomach.

As Tommy struggled for air, Hunter bent down over him.

'Listen to me, you idiot,' he hissed, waving the cudgel in front of Tommy's face. 'If you ever, *ever* lead the police anywhere near here, you'll get something a lot sharper than this in your guts. You got that?'

Tommy tried to nod, but a lump of semi-chewed pizza had become stuck in his throat and all he could do was make a harsh, choking sound. He was aware of Hunter standing up and addressing the rest of the kids in the room.

'The same goes for the rest of you,' the man shouted. 'Anybody got a problem with that?'

Nobody replied. They wouldn't dare. Like Tommy, they all hated Hunter. But in return for a daily stream of stolen cash, he gave them something they needed. A roof over their heads. Food. And something more important than both of these: safety in numbers. Because when you worked the streets, there was nothing more important than that.

It was 9 a.m. exactly when Felix returned. Ricky's bed was untouched. He hadn't moved from the sofa. Thirty playing cards were spread out in front of him. He stared at them for fifteen seconds. Then he closed his eyes. 'Queen of hearts,' he said. 'Two of spades, five of diamonds, nine of clubs . . .'

Thirty seconds later, he had recited the name of every card in order. He opened his eyes again. Felix was leaning on his walking stick and staring at him carefully.

'Very good, Coco,' he murmured. 'Really very good. Perhaps we'll make something of you yet.'

Ricky smiled. 'It's just a party game, though. That's all.'

'We'll see,' Felix said slyly. 'We'll see.'

But inside Ricky's head, another conversation was taking place, this one with Ziggy.

– You've won him over. That's good. Let's keep it that way. The things he's teaching you will be useful on the street. Learn what you can from him. Improve yourself.

– And when the time comes to leave?

– Then you leave.

PART TWO

PART TWO

7

WEAPONS

The weeks that followed passed quickly. Ricky's days were full and there was no time at all for him to spend the £100 living allowance that Felix handed over every Saturday morning. Not that he needed the money. Every time he left the flat, he returned to find the fridge full, his clothes cleaned and the flat tidy. He never saw the person – or people – responsible. When he mentioned it, Felix had simply said, 'You haven't got time for housework,' and refused to discuss it any more.

So each week, Ricky squirrelled his money away, inside a sock which he kept under the mattress. It would come in useful, he told himself, for when he finally walked out of there.

But Felix wasn't wrong. There *was* no time for anything else other than his lessons. He turned up every morning at 9 a.m. exactly, peering across the threshold and politely asking if he could come in. Once inside, he worked Ricky hard.

A couple of hours of every morning were spent in the gym, which was housed in one of the spare rooms of the flat. There were several weight machines, an exercise bike and even a treadmill. Ricky grew to hate that treadmill. He'd have been happy to bulk up with some bicep curls or shoulder presses, but Felix soon stamped on that idea. 'You're not fully-grown yet, so you could damage your body with too many weights. You need aerobic fitness, so get running on the treadmill.'

'Don't see you doing it,' Ricky had replied grumpily.

'Count the legs, Coco. Besides, I've done my stint of vomiting my guts out through exercise. Now it's your turn.' He'd picked a chunk of peanut brittle out of his sweet bag

And Ricky *was* sick, several times. It didn't seem to worry Felix, who watched without expression as he doubled over, retching. But as the weeks flew past, he found he could run for longer and longer, at higher speeds. He even found himself looking forward to those daily training sessions, though he'd never have admitted that to Felix. He had also had his hair cut – his long hair had kept sticking to his neck and it was far cooler to run with a shorter, if still scruffy, style. And that haircut was just about the only thing he'd had time to spend any money on.

His brain had as much exercise as his body. After two weeks he could memorize half a pack of cards in fifteen seconds. After four weeks he could do a whole pack in thirty. 'Not bad, huh?' he said to Felix the first time he managed that feat. Somehow, a word of approval from Felix was beginning to *matter*.

Felix had shrugged. 'It's a start,' he said.

But from then on, Ricky's lessons in observation became even trickier. The following day, Felix led him out of the apartment and down a nearby main road. As they walked side by side, he said, suddenly, 'What was the registration plate of the red Mini that just passed?'

Ricky blinked at him. 'What do you mean?'

'How do you think this works, Coco? You think that in real life someone's going to spread out a pack of cards and ask you where the nine of clubs is? You need your eyes open and your brain in record mode *all the time*. You need to see everything. Remember everything. You were right when you said counting cards is just a party game. This' – he stopped for a moment and rapped his walking stick on the pavement – 'is real life.'

They walked on in silence for another thirty seconds.

'Blue Peugeot,' Felix said suddenly. 'What's the—'

'RE75 UHF.'

If Felix was impressed, he didn't show it. 'We passed a betting shop thirty seconds ago,' he replied immediately. 'There was a man standing outside smoking a cigarette. What colour was his hair?'

Ricky blinked again. 'I thought we were doing number plates.'

Felix raised an eyebrow. 'You need to see *everything*,' he repeated.

And from that moment onwards, whenever they were out, Felix would fire impossible questions at Ricky. He would ask him the colour of someone's tie a minute after they'd walked past. How many people were sitting outside a café 100 metres behind them? What had been advertised on the side of a London bus that had now driven out of sight?

At first Felix's constant questions were infuriating. After two weeks they were simply annoying. But gradually, Ricky found he was getting used not only to the questions, but also to remembering the smallest details of everything he saw. As he grew more accomplished at it, the world seemed like a different place, full of activity that he'd never have noticed beforehand. He counted pigeons sitting on telegraph wires, noticed the facial expressions of everyone who came into his field of view, even subconsciously catalogued the litter that they passed on the pavement. 'You'll be amazed,' Felix told him one day, as his ability to observe grew, 'how often the ability to notice and recall something very small can make the difference between life and death.'

Life and death?

Ricky didn't like it when Felix used words like that. He wasn't here to worry about life and death. Didn't really want even to know what Felix was all about. Whenever his mind drifted towards that subject, he'd stopped himself thinking about it too hard. He was here to learn what he could, and then apply it to become a better thief. Simple. And seeing and remembering what other people missed would certainly help him do that.

'I bet you're not much of a fighter,' Felix said one day as Ricky stepped off the treadmill, sweat trickling down his forehead, his T-shirt soaked. It was raining hard outside. Great clouds of rain were visible over the river from the window of the penthouse flat. Felix had arrived with a soaked rucksack over his shoulder and an umbrella which he had propped up by the door. But he didn't look like he'd been using the umbrella – his clothes and balding head were soaked.

Ricky eyed him suspiciously. Yesterday, Felix had rocked up with a dirty black bin liner full of rotting rubbish and a pair of thick rubber gloves. 'Trash!' he had announced with a smile. 'You'll be amazed what sort of information you can find by rummaging through people's bins.' Ricky had spent the next hour sorting through the stinking debris inside the bag, trying to work out what might be useful, and what might not. He found a stained old telephone bill and a bank statement, which Felix agreed would be priceless if you were trying to find out about the person who'd discarded them. As for the old baked bean cans and dirty nappies: not so much.

'I said,' Felix repeated, 'that I bet you're not much of a fighter.'

'Well, I'm a brilliant bin man,' Ricky replied sourly.

'Don't get touchy.' Felix was in a strange mood today – probably because his clothes were still damp.

'It's better to run than fight, anyway,' Ricky said.

'Much better,' Felix agreed. 'But sometimes we don't have a choice. Sometimes we have to defend ourselves.'

'You're the one that doesn't want me doing weights.'

'Correct,' said Felix. 'But good fighting isn't always about strength. Sometimes it's about technique.'

'I had karate lessons once,' Ricky said. 'I was rubbish at them.'

'I'm not talking about karate,' said Felix. 'Oh, I'm sure it's all very well, but the best advice I can give you is this: if you find yourself in a fight with someone, forget all the fancy stuff. Get your hands on something very heavy and hit them over the head with it.'

Ricky stared at him, as if to say: *Is that the best advice you can give me?*

Felix seemed not to notice. 'Of course, sometimes you *can't* get your hands on something heavy, which means you have to improvise. Want to see one of the best weapons you can carry around with you?'

'Uzi nine millimetre?' Ricky suggested. He meant it as a joke, and was a bit taken aback when Felix seemed to take him perfectly seriously.

'Not my weapon of choice. Too much of a recoil kick, and too flashy by half. Try walking down the street with an Uzi and you'll stick out like a—'

'Like a kid with a sub-machine gun?'

'Well, exactly. The time might come, Coco, when you and I have a serious conversation about firearms and other weapons. But even the organization

I work for would think twice about putting firearms in the hands of kids.'

It was the first time Felix had ever mentioned such an organization. Ricky didn't question him any further. He could tell when Felix was on a roll.

'Glad to hear it,' he said instead. 'Guns aren't really my style.'

'It's not a question of style, Coco,' Felix said irritably. 'It's a question of what's practical. You can't easily carry a firearm or a knife around with you without attracting all sorts of unwanted attention. Much better to carry one of these.' He started patting himself down. 'Now, where did I put it? Ah, here it is!' He put his hand in his back pocket and pulled out a pen.

'Er, no, Felix, that's a pen.'

'Yep. Good one too,' Felix said. 'Cartier. A gift from a colleague of mine called Michael. I never leave home without it.'

– Is he joking?

Ricky peered at his mentor. He *looked* pretty serious.

'What am I supposed to do with that?' Ricky asked. 'Squirt ink in someone's eye?'

'It's a ballpoint, Coco,' said Felix in a withering tone of voice. 'Want to know how to use it, or are

you going to be too busy making clever comments?'
Felix really *was* in a mood.

'I want to know how to use it,' Ricky said quietly.

Felix nodded. 'Good.' He sniffed. 'A pen is a good
example of an improvised weapon,' he said. 'An
improvised weapon needs to be something you can
carry around with you that *looks* absolutely harm-
less – something nobody would ever *think* of as
a weapon, but which is strong and sturdy enough
to be used in self-defence.' He dug his free hand
into his pocket and pulled out a handful of change.
'Coins,' he said. 'A very good example. Everyone
carries them and nobody thinks they're dangerous.
But if I throw a handful of coins hard enough at
your face, believe me, you're going to know
about it.'

Ricky winced slightly at the thought. 'Point
taken,' he said.

Felix returned the change to his pocket, then held
up the pen again. 'I suppose we'd better get this over
with,' he muttered. 'Punch me, please.'

'What?'

'Punch me.'

'Really?'

'I'm afraid so. Hard as you can.'

Reluctantly, Ricky stepped up to where Felix was
standing. Half a metre between them. He looked at

the floor, then suddenly swung out his right arm with his fist clenched, aiming for Felix's jaw.

Not for the first time, Felix's agility surprised him. He lifted up his left arm in a quick, deft movement to block Ricky's right hook. As he did this, he used his pen hand to stab at the soft flesh on the inside of Ricky's elbow joint.

'*Ow!*' Ricky shouted. '*That hurt!*'

Felix's brow was furrowed and there were beads of sweat on his bald head. He mopped them off with the palm of his free hand. 'Yeah, sorry about that,' he said mildly. 'Would you like a sw—'

'*NO! I WOULDN'T LIKE A SWEET!*'

'It *was* kind of *meant* to hurt,' Felix continued. 'Soft flesh, you see. Always the most tender place to go for. If I'd struck a bit harder, I could have put you down for up to a minute. And then, of course, there's the neck . . .'

Ricky found himself involuntarily shielding his neck with the palm of his hand. There was something about the mournful way Felix was explaining all this that freaked him out.

Felix dropped the pen onto the coffee table, then turned round and stomped over to where his rucksack and umbrella were leaning against the wall. He picked them up and carried them back to Ricky.

'Brolly,' he said. 'Awesome weapon. Good solid

spike at one end, and a bit of heft in the pole, if you get a good old-fashioned one that's made of wood.'

'I suppose you'd like to whack me over the head with it?'

Felix's brow creased even more. 'I *am* sorry about the pen, Coco. But I did need to demonstrate. I think you get the idea with the umbrella, though.' He dropped the brolly onto the floor, then started rummaging in his rucksack. 'Here we go,' he said, before pulling out a chunky hardback book.

Ricky caught sight of the cover. It read: *War and Peace*. 'More homework?' he asked.

'Eh?' Felix looked at the cover himself. 'Oh God, no – very long, very boring.' He held the book up with the spine facing outwards. 'Have a close look.'

Ricky walked up to take the book. But as he approached, Felix jabbed the spine of the book so hard against his neck that Ricky felt his knees tremble and collapse beneath him.

'*OW!*' he shouted for the second time that morning, and clutched his pulsing neck.

'Ah . . .' Felix said. 'Sorry . . . sorry . . . perhaps I hit you a bit harder than I meant to . . . but you get the point?'

Ricky tried to explain that he got the point very well, but all that came out was a kind of strangled gurgling.

'I must say, though,' Felix continued, examining the book a little more closely, 'there *is* a good solid spine on this one. *War and Peace*. I'll have to remember that. I used *Harry Potter and the Chamber of Secrets* the other week, and that was rubbish.' He jabbed it against his free hand a few times, then looked at Ricky again, who was still gasping on his knees. 'Here,' he said, 'let me help you up. You look a bit unwell.'

Ricky staggered to his feet. 'Have you got any more surprises for me?' he gasped.

'Well, actually . . .' Felix replied. He rummaged in his rucksack again and pulled out a newspaper. 'This morning's *Times*,' he said.

Ricky was still rubbing his neck. He peered at Felix. 'You're joking, right?'

'Not at all. Very effective weapon, a newspaper. Watch.'

Felix sat down at the coffee table and started folding the newspaper in half, then in half again. After several folds he had a thick, sturdy truncheon of paper. He swiped it gently through the air, as if weighing up its heft. Then, very suddenly, he slammed it against the table. Ricky started. He looked at the coffee table to check that the glass hadn't cracked. It was still OK, but that didn't put his mind at rest. 'Tell me you're not going to try that thing on me,' he said.

'Of course not,' Felix said. He sounded slightly hurt. Then he whacked the truncheon against the coffee table again. And yet again, Ricky started. It was quite obvious that Felix's makeshift truncheon could do someone a lot of damage. 'Would you like a go?' Felix asked him.

Ricky held out his hand and grabbed the truncheon as Felix got to his feet. It felt solid in his fist as he tapped it a few times against the palm of his free hand.

'Try and hit me with it,' Felix said, hitching the rucksack over one shoulder.

This morning was getting crazier by the moment. 'Why?' Ricky asked.

'Just try it, Coco.'

'I don't want to hurt you.' He was sarcastic.

'I promise not to cry.'

Ricky sighed. He looked at the floor. Then, with a sudden movement, he stepped towards Felix and raised the truncheon. When he was half a metre away, he started to bring it down towards Felix's head.

Once again, Felix took Ricky by surprise. The older man twisted his rucksack shoulder towards him, and with one hand raised the rucksack itself. As Ricky brought the truncheon down, it hit the rucksack harmlessly. In another quick movement, Felix removed the pack from his shoulder. He flipped it so that the flaps were facing outwards, then deftly slung them over Ricky's head. With one strong arm he twisted Ricky's body so that he was facing away from him, the strap of the rucksack crossing his Adam's apple.

Then he pulled. Tightly.

For the second time that morning, Ricky found himself struggling for air. He dropped the truncheon and tried to grab the straps to pull them away from his neck, but Felix's grip on the rucksack was too firm.

He started to feel dizzy.

His knees went weak.

He was going to faint . . .

Only when he was sinking to the floor did Felix release the rucksack. Ricky fell to his knees as he inhaled several noisy lungfuls of air. Felix stood above him, an embarrassed frown on his face. He stretched out one hand to help Ricky to his feet.

'Are you OK?'

'No!' Ricky rasped. 'I nearly passed out!'

Felix nodded. 'Yes,' he said. 'I suppose that could happen.' He looked around the room at the pen, the book, the newspaper and the rucksack in his arms. 'Improvising,' he said. 'Very important. Forget knives and guns. Most of the time we just have to use the tools that are available to us. Here, you can have this.' He handed Ricky the rucksack and limped towards the exit. 'I think that's about enough for today,' he said. 'I'll be back tomorrow. We'll start learning about surveillance. Very important technique for a soldier.'

'What do you mean, *for a soldier*?' Ricky gasped. '*You're* the soldier, not me.'

Felix smiled. Then he pulled his ever-present bag of sweets from his pocket and popped one in his mouth. 'If you say so,' he said, before turning his back on the sore and battered Ricky, and leaving the room.

8

SURVEILLANCE

'Meet Scruffy,' Felix said the following day when he turned up at his usual time. He handed Ricky a small, creased photograph of a golden Labrador with big, sad eyes. When Ricky gave him a confused look, he added: 'Scruffy's your dog.'

'What are you talking about? I don't have a dog.'

Felix gave him one of his infuriatingly smug smiles. 'I know you don't have a dog,' he said. '*You* know you don't have a dog. But the man in the street doesn't.'

Felix was being even more obscure than usual. 'I suppose you are going to get around to telling me what you're talking about?' Ricky said.

'It's very simple,' said Felix. 'Stick that picture of Scruffy in your wallet. Sometimes, when you're conducting surveillance on a person or location, you have to loiter in the same place for a long time. That attracts people's attention. If someone challenges you, all you need to do is pull out your picture of Scruffy and show it to them. Say you were walking your dog in the area and it got away from you. Now you're just hanging around for a bit on the off-chance that it comes back to the same place. If you can manage to look a bit tearful about the whole affair, so much the better. Oh, and we mustn't forget to teach you how to fix your bike.'

'Fix my bike?'

'Yeah, of course. Best cover in the world. Nobody looks twice at a cyclist fiddling with his chain. It means you can stay in the same place, watching and waiting, for ages. But you need to be doing proper repairs, because if anybody's watching you who knows anything about bikes and they see you're faking it, they'll know it's just a pretence.'

'And you think that'll happen a lot, do you?' Ricky said. 'People watching me watching them.' He was *seriously* beginning to wonder what he had let himself in for now.

Felix suddenly looked very sober. 'Yes,' he said. 'In our world, Coco, everybody's watching every-body else. You need to become very, *very* good at it.'

'Let me guess, you're the guy to teach me?'

'Well, as it happens . . .' Felix said, and he gave a little mock bow.

Half an hour later, they had started with the basics.

'You need to know how to follow someone in a crowd, without them *knowing* that you're following.'

Ricky looked around. It was ten in the morning, a cold, slightly damp early December day. They were standing outside a shoe shop on Oxford Street. The area was busy with Christmas shoppers eager to make use of the final few shopping weeks before the big day. Ricky himself was glad to have something to keep his mind off all that. For an orphan living on his own, there's nothing festive about Christmas.

'Are you paying attention, Coco?'

'Sure. Following someone in a crowd.'

'That's right. Now, you'll learn the first thing you need to know about surveillance in here.' He rapped on the window of the shoe shop.

'Er, no, that's a shoe shop, Felix.'

'You bet it is. The feet are the key,' Felix said. 'An amateur will make a note of their target's jumper or coat, or even worse they'll keep their eyes fixed on the back of their target's head.'

'What's wrong with that?'

Felix gave him a look that seemed to say: *Do I really have to tell you?* 'If you're looking at the back of someone's head, as soon as they turn round they'll see you looking straight at them. Easiest way to get noticed. Much better to look at their shoes. Look how many different styles of shoe there are just in this one shop window. A hundred, maybe more? People's shoes are *always* very distinctive, so if you follow them it makes it easy to keep track of where they are. Plus, if they turn round, you look like you have your eyes on the pavement. It makes it much harder for them to spot you. Now, look at my shoes, and remember them.'

Felix was wearing a pair of scruffy but comfortable Nike Airs. If you didn't know that he had a prosthetic leg, you certainly wouldn't be able to tell if all you could see was his feet.

Ricky spent the next few hours following his mentor. The walking stick made it easier, of course, but after a while Ricky found himself getting into a rhythm. He kept a distance of about ten metres as Felix walked in and out of department stores, up escalators and down quiet side streets. Every now and then, Ricky made the mistake of raising his eyes and looking at Felix's body rather than just his shoes. It was as if Felix himself knew when this was going to happen. Without exception, Ricky's mentor would turn and stare directly into his eyes, before making a gesture that Ricky found very unnerving: a slicing sign with his forefinger across the front of his throat. Ricky didn't know quite what it meant, but it always encouraged him to redouble his efforts.

Soon, Ricky found that he was starting to enjoy himself as Felix made things more difficult – changing direction halfway down a street, or jumping on a bus and forcing Ricky to follow as covertly as possible. It was a challenge that he was up to, he decided as he followed those scruffy Nike Airs along Piccadilly and into Green Park. He'd been good at following people even before he'd met Felix. Now he was—

'*Ouch!*'

Both Ricky and Felix said it at the same time, and with good reason. Ricky had walked straight into his mentor's back, and the collision had hurt.

Felix turned. 'It was only a matter of time before you did that,' he said.

'What do you mean?'

'You were daydreaming, Coco. But even worse, you weren't paying attention to how fast or slow I was walking. Sometimes you were ten metres behind me, sometimes more, sometimes less. That's OK if it's what you mean to do, but if you don't . . .' He slammed his two palms together, and Ricky blinked as he did it. 'Bang! And if you're following a professional . . .'

'A professional what?'

'. . . they'll be adjusting their pace. Short strides,

long strides – they'll mix it up as a way of finding out if anyone's tailing them. You need to follow their stride. That way, *you* control the distance between you both, not them.' Felix pointed towards a nearby park bench. 'Let's sit down,' he said. 'My leg's killing me.'

'So what you're saying,' Ricky said as they sat down, 'is that I didn't do very well.'

'Actually,' Felix replied, 'you did brilliantly. Pear drop?'

'No thanks.'

'You're not one for sweets, are you?'

'Not pear drops, anyway.'

'What's your favourite?'

'I dunno. Smarties?'

Felix made a face, as though Smarties were the most disgusting thing that had ever been invented, then popped a pear drop into his mouth. 'Anyway, like I was saying, you did very well. But we need to take you to the next level. Following someone from behind is all very well, but if you're conducting surveillance on a target who thinks someone might be watching, they'll notice you sooner or later.'

Ricky gave Felix a confused look. 'Well, if I can't follow someone from behind . . .' His voice trailed off.

'If you can't follow someone from behind, Coco, then you have to follow them from in front.'

'But that doesn't make any sense.'

'Sure it does. If you think you're being followed, you're going to look over your shoulder, not up ahead.'

'But you've *got* to be behind someone to follow them. That's what following *means*.'

Felix smiled. 'Not in our world,' he said. He winced as he got to his feet and put pressure on his bad leg. 'Come on, I'll show you.'

It was hard. Much harder than following from behind. Felix explained how to use the reflections in shop windows, or the wing mirrors of cars driving along the street, to keep an eye on his mark. But the shop windows were already filled with glittering Christmas displays, which made it difficult to focus on the reflections, and the vehicles moved in stops and starts, their mirrors obscured by the swarming crowds.

Ricky kept complaining that this was an impossible task. Felix listened with a mild smile. Then he made him continue practising. He taught him how to cross the road and walk just in front of the target, casting only the occasional sidelong glance to make sure they were still in his sights. By the end of that first day Ricky was nowhere near competent. But Felix made him practise, every day for the following week, and the week after that.

As the days passed, the weather grew colder. The rain turned to snow, and the snow to slush, which became covered in snow again. Ricky got used to his shoes and the bottoms of his trousers being perpetually wet as he tramped through the dirty, sludgy streets. But somehow he didn't mind, because gradually he could feel his skills improving. He found that he could walk twenty metres ahead of Felix and be quite confident that he knew where his mentor was. It was like a sixth sense, and it grew stronger with each hour that passed.

'When you're following someone, you also need to make sure you pay attention to what *you're* wearing,' Felix explained on Christmas Eve morning as they were walking from the apartment to continue their practice. A thin drizzle of snow had just started to fall. 'Make sure it's appropriate to where you are. If you're in a rough, poor area, wearing all the latest designer gear will make you stick out like a sore thumb. Likewise if you look like an urchin in Mayfair. And one of these is a good idea.'

From the pocket of his coat he pulled out a baseball cap.

'If you think your target has spotted you, put on a baseball cap. It changes your features immediately. You can wear it forwards, backwards and even' – he punched the cap so that the red inside became the outside – 'inside out. This one's invertible. Very useful.' He propped the baseball cap on Ricky's head as they turned a corner into Regent Street. 'Keeps your head warm too,' he murmured.

The smell of roasting chestnuts wafted under Ricky's nose. He felt a pang. It was such a Christmassy smell. And with the snow, and the Regent Street lights, and the shoppers with their bags full of Christmas gifts, it was such a Christmassy sight.

– *Everyone's looking forward to being with their family. Except us.*

– *Get used to it. We don't have any family any more.*

It was true. The closest thing Ricky had to it right now was a strange one-legged ex-army intelligence officer whose sole purpose in life seemed to be to turn him into the best-trained pickpocket in London. In a strange way, though, he was grateful for that. It kept his mind off everything he was missing.

He turned to Felix and smiled. 'What now?' he asked.

Felix clapped his hands briskly together. 'I'm going for a wander,' he announced. 'I'll meet you back here in three hours. I want you tell me where I've been and what I've done. If I've eaten a sandwich for lunch, I want you to tell me what the filling was. And if I *see* you . . .'

'I know, I know,' said Ricky, and before Felix could do it himself, he made the slicing gesture across his throat.

'Turkey and stuffing from Pret a Manger. Chocolate brownie. Black coffee, three sugars. You should cut down on the sugar, Felix. You'll have no teeth left.'

'Thanks for the advice, pipsqueak. And good work with the surveillance. I didn't see you once. Come on, it's five o'clock and I'm freezing. Let's get you home.'

The underground was very crowded, so although it was suddenly bitterly cold outside, Ricky felt sweaty and dirty by the time they were standing outside his apartment block. 'Have tomorrow off,' Felix said.

Another time, Ricky might have replied with a sarcastic comment. Tonight he looked up to the top of the apartment block, which was almost hidden in the swirling snow. 'I could make you a cup of tea or something,' he said quietly.

Felix shook his head. 'I'm sorry, Coco,' he said. 'I've got family waiting for me.'

Ricky felt himself blush. He frowned and looked at his shoes. 'Right,' he said. 'Of course. Sorry.'

Somehow he'd never thought of Felix as having a family.

'Here,' Felix said. He pulled a small paper bag from his pocket and handed it to Ricky. It was still warm. Ricky looked inside. It was a bag of the roasted chestnuts that had smelled so good. 'Happy Christmas.'

'Yeah,' Ricky said quietly. 'You too.'

'Rest up,' Felix said. 'You've still got a long way to go. We start again on Boxing Day.'

There was no 'Well done'. No 'Happy Christmas, Coco'. Without another word, Felix turned and walked away.

'I might go out,' Ricky shouted. 'Celebrate by myself.' He knew he was being petulant, but somehow he couldn't help it.

Felix stopped and turned. 'Stay home, Coco,' he said. 'That's an order.' Then he turned and limped off into the snow.

Ricky burned with anger. He dug his hands into his pockets and tramped into the foyer of the apartment block.

Was anybody about to have a worse Christmas than him? he wondered.

9

THE BLEAK MIDWINTER

When she was younger, Izzy Cole had loved these days before Christmas.

She especially liked the evenings, when it was dark outside, maybe even snowing. There was always an enormous Christmas tree in the large entrance hall of the White House. She would sit for hours and stare at its twinkling lights. There would be Christmas carols playing in the background, and amazing smells wafting from the kitchen where their housekeeper was baking goodies for her.

This year, the Christmas tree was just as large and beautifully decorated as before. The Christmas songs drifted in the air. But there was nothing cosy or festive about the house that evening, because all Izzy could hear was the screaming.

It had started that afternoon. As Izzy walked past

her father's office, she'd heard him shouting down the phone. '*You won't get a single thing, Dmitri, until I get my money!*'

The sickening thought immediately struck Izzy that he was talking about something crooked or dodgy. There had been something in his voice that had chilled her. A horrible mixture of greed and anger. And fear, maybe. Yes, there was definitely fear somewhere in the mix.

Now, as she listened to her parents arguing, the greed and fear had left his voice, but the anger hadn't.

She didn't know what they were arguing about. But it sounded bad, because even her mum, who was normally too scared of her dad to disagree with him, was shouting. Izzy sat beneath the Christmas tree, her knees up against her chest, her hands clasped over her ears, trying to block out the sound. But she couldn't. Her parents' screams rose above the strains of 'In the Bleak Midwinter'.

Suddenly she stood up. She couldn't take it any more. She stormed across the entrance hall and burst into the drawing room, where her mum and dad were yelling at each other. Her dad was standing just inside the door with that look on his face that normally warned Izzy to keep her distance from him. Her mum was on the other side of the room opposite the fire. Her face was wet with tears, and make-up streamed down her cheeks.

'Shut up!' Izzy shouted. 'Just *shut up*! *Shut u*—'

She was silenced by her father's fist. He swiped her across her face with the back of his big hand, harder than he'd ever hit her before. Izzy collapsed, too shocked and stunned to cry. She touched her nose and saw that her fingertips were smeared with blood.

Her father stood over her, a hot anger in his eyes, the hand with which he'd hit her still raised. For an awful moment she thought he was going to strike her again, but then he lowered his hand, turned his back on Izzy and her mother and stormed out of the room.

There was a horrible silence. The carriage clock on the mantelpiece chimed 10 p.m. as Izzy wiped the stream of blood from her nose, then looked over at her mum. Her mum's eyes were raw from crying, and there seemed to be the beginnings of a bruise on her face. Izzy staggered to her feet and was just about to run across the room to hug her mother, when she saw something in her face that stopped her. It was a little curl of the lip. A sneer. Izzy's mum was looking at her daughter with contempt.

'You *stupid* girl,' she hissed. 'You *stupid*, *stupid* girl. Why did you make him do that?'

Izzy stood very still and stared at her mother.

'It's your fault,' her mum continued. 'All this is *your* fault. We were *fine* before you came along.'

'He hit me, Mum,' Izzy whispered.

'Well, you probably deserved it,' her mother snapped as she hurried away from the fireplace towards the door. As she passed Izzy, she gave her another horrible look. 'You should just keep your mouth shut, you stupid little girl,' she said, before disappearing from the room.

Izzy stood alone, blood still pouring from her nose. Her face hurt, but her body and her mind were numb. She stared into the middle distance, unable to believe what had just happened. The music changed. 'Silent Night'.

She made her decision there and then.

Izzy turned and, with her sleeve up against her nose to stem the flow of blood, left the room. There was no sign of her parents in the hallway. Good. She walked past the twinkling Christmas tree and up the stairs. In a little corner of her mind she half expected her mum to be in her bedroom, waiting to apologize. But she wasn't, and that just made Izzy even more determined to go ahead with her plan.

There was a black rucksack under her bed which she normally used for school trips. She pulled it out and filled it with handfuls of clean underwear, a deodorant and a toothbrush and toothpaste. She looked out of the window. The snow was falling heavier than before, settling thickly on the stone statues dotted around their large gardens. She would need warm clothes. She found her thickest jumper, a pair of gloves and a woollen hat, before putting on an extra pair of socks and her leather walking boots.

She had just under forty pounds, which she stuffed into her pocket, before looking around her room one last time. It was a warm, comfortable room. A haven from the horrible things that happened elsewhere in the house. But she really couldn't stay here any more.

She looked in the mirror. The bleeding had stopped, but her lips and skin were stained with blood and her face was throbbing. She cleaned herself up with a moisturizing wipe, swallowed a couple of painkillers, then shouldered her rucksack and stepped up to the door.

She put her ear to the door and listened carefully. There was no noise, so she slowly opened the door and looked out. The landing was clear, and so were the stairs. She crept out and tiptoed down to the hallway.

She couldn't leave by the main entrance. There was a video camera there that recorded everything.

Instead, she crept past the Christmas tree, deeply breathing in its festive scent, and slowly opened the door which led to the kitchen. There was a tray of cakes on the side, and something simmering on the stove. But their cook wasn't there, so Izzy swiftly slipped in.

Aside from the back door, and the door that led into the pantry, there was one other door from the kitchen; it led into a small box room to one side. Inside this room, Izzy knew, there was a bank of closed-circuit television screens. Her father was obsessed with security, and every part of the exterior of the house was covered by a security camera.

Or so he thought.

The cameras fed directly to this room and anyone in there could watch the comings and goings of the house. The video feeds were constantly recorded. Sometimes there was a security person there to monitor them in real time. But Izzy had known, ever since she was old enough to play in the garden by herself, that not *every* part of the garden was covered by those cameras. It was possible to get from the kitchen door to the wall at the bottom of the garden – admittedly by a very roundabout route – without appearing on those little monitors off the kitchen. One of her favourite games as a child had been to see how secretly she could complete that route. She'd never thought that her little game would become useful.

A key to the kitchen door was in its usual place in one of the cutlery drawers. Izzy grabbed it, then headed to the back door, pausing only to stuff a few of the little cakes – not enough to be missed – into her pack.

She stopped.

What did she think she was doing, running away into the freezing, snowy night? She wouldn't last a day.

Her shoulders slumped in defeat. She almost turned to go back to her room.

But then she caught sight of her reflection in the glass of the door. Pale. Frightened. Bruised. Bleeding. It reminded her that she would be no less safe on the streets than here at home.

She took a deep breath, unlocked the door and stepped outside.

The air and the swirling blizzard stung her face – it was much colder than she had expected. There was at least five centimetres of snow on the ground, which meant there was no way she could avoid leaving footprints. At least, she thought to herself, the swirling snow would hide them from anybody looking out of the window, and would cover them up soon enough.

She closed and locked the door behind her.

Rather than head directly towards the gate at the bottom of the garden, she turned immediately right and started weaving her way round some snow-covered flower beds. After a minute, she came to the old swing that she hadn't used for years. Here she turned left again and, keeping to the edge of the small vegetable patch where the large winter cabbages were laden with snow, she crept towards the brick wall at the bottom of the garden. It was about three metres high and covered with a sturdy vine. In the summer, its leaves covered the whole wall, but now it was nothing but bare, strong branches. Along the top of the wall she knew there was a line of barbed wire to deter intruders, but it was covered now in several centimetres of snow.

There was a gate another five metres to her left, but Izzy knew the cameras were watching it. This part of the wall, though, was a blind spot. She grabbed a fistful of vine branch. It creaked slightly, but held her weight as she used it to climb up the wall. She didn't want to disturb the snow on the top of the wall or, more importantly, get tangled in the barbed wire. So as she reached the top, she flung her legs athletically over the wall. A little cloud of powder sprayed in the air as she vaulted over.

She landed on the other side of the wall in a

painful, crumpled heap, but she quickly stood up again. She was in the narrow alleyway that ran behind the White House, and for a moment she hesitated. She stared at the kitchen key in the palm of her gloved hand. If she kept hold of it, she could at least creep back inside the house if she changed her mind.

'But I *won't* be changing my mind,' she whispered to herself. So she let the key fall. It disappeared into the snow at her feet.

Izzy checked her watch. Eleven p.m. One hour till Christmas, she thought to herself as she looked both ways down the alley. Left or right? she wondered.

It didn't really matter. Either direction would take her away from the White House and out into the streets of London. She certainly couldn't stay with friends. The very first thing their parents would do was call Izzy's mum and dad. She'd be back in hell before she knew it.

No. From now on, the streets were going to be her home.

Eleven p.m.

Ricky had never seen a blizzard like it. From his warm penthouse apartment he watched it swirl so thickly over the city that the skyline was barely visible. The light on the top of Canary Wharf flashed dimly, and he could just make out the vague silhouette of London Bridge.

He'd tried watching telly. As soon as he'd switched it on, there had been an advert for powdered gravy. A family sitting around their Christmas meal, all smiles and happiness. Ricky couldn't watch. He had immediately switched off the telly and stared into space, thinking about his mum and dad, and of course his sister Madeleine.

She had been older than him. Nearly sixteen when their parents had died. After the car crash, she had been sent to a different set of foster parents to Ricky. They had treated her badly. Very badly. Ricky found his temperature rising at the thought of it, and for the first time since he had been off the streets, he dug out the precious letter she had written him:

Dearest Ricky,
I know you won't understand what I'm about to do, but you have to believe me when I say it's for the best. These people they've sent me to live with are the worst. I've got bruises all up my arms and along my back, and I just can't take it any more . . .

But as usual, he couldn't bear to read to the end.

Fighting back tears, he tucked the letter into its envelope and went back to staring into space.

He couldn't stop thinking about his big sister. She had been so *kind*. The year before their parents had died, it had been Madeleine who insisted that they spend their Christmas Eve working at a soup kitchen. That was the kind of person she was. Always thinking about other people. Not like Ricky, who was always thinking about himself.

– *Stop feeling sorry for yourself. Life isn't so bad. Look around you. This is better than Baxter's, isn't it?*

– *Yeah, but why am I here? The streets are full of kids like me.*

– *Compassion, Ricky? Don't let it get the better of you. Look at the scar on your wrist. The Thrownaways did that, remember? They aren't quite like you.*

Ricky ignored his inner voice. He was suddenly angry. Angry with the world, and angry with Felix. He felt like disobeying him, like doing something he wouldn't approve of, but that his older sister *would*.

And doing it now.

He grabbed the rucksack Felix had given him and strode into the kitchen. As usual, the fridge was full of food. A whole cooked chicken. Bags of apples and oranges. Cans of Coke. Ready-made salads. Cakes. More than he could eat, and he knew the fridge would soon be replenished anyway. He paused a moment as he spotted some special Christmassy food – a packet of mince pies, a pud, a tray of Christmas veggies ready to zap in the microwave. A bit of Christmas cheer from Felix, then . . . But it didn't stop him. He stuffed the rucksack full of food and drinks, then put on a warm hooded top and grabbed a fistful of notes from the sock under his mattress. He slung the rucksack over his shoulder. On a sideboard in the hallway, he saw the knife that Felix had confiscated from the druggie woman in Bloomsbury Square. Next to it, a ballpoint pen.

His fingers hovered over the knife for a few seconds. But he didn't touch it. Madeleine wouldn't approve. Instead, he grabbed the pen and shoved it in his pocket. Then he left the flat.

Outside the apartment block, he tramped through the snow. It took five minutes for his feet and hands to go numb, but he kept walking. Only after another ten minutes did he see the orange of a black cab's 'For Hire' sign. He flagged it down, and when the driver pulled up alongside him and lowered his window, shouted, 'King's Cross.'

The driver was a white-haired man in his sixties, and he didn't look very cheerful. 'You got money, kid?'

Ricky pushed back his hood, put his hand in

his pocket and held up two twenty-pound notes. The cab driver nodded, and Ricky climbed into the back.

It was blissfully warm in the cab. His breath misted the windows as they drove along the river, then north up Kingsway. The driver didn't speak as they drove, and Ricky was glad about that because there was already a conversation going on in his head.

– *You're crazy. The Thrownaways will be cold and hungry. They'll go for you.*

– *I don't care. It's Christmas. Why should I have all this food and everybody else go hungry? Anyway, I'm not Felix's little pet. I don't have to stay home and do what he says.*

The fare came to £35. Ricky stepped out in front of King's Cross station and waited for the grumpy cab driver to pull away. He checked his watch. Five minutes to midnight. The main road was still busy but the pavements were emptying fast and fresh snow had settled on the slush. He scanned the surrounding area, and found his mind instantly recording everything he saw. A number 63 bus heading west. A couple on the opposite side of the road, arm in arm, battling their way through the snow. Two police officers in fluorescent hi-viz jackets surveying the traffic. A girl in a woollen hat heading for the main road. Two drunks staggering towards the station . . .

He was facing a dark side street. Dustbins on either side. Only one street lamp working, and that was flickering with a dim yellow light. The snow was falling more heavily than ever and he could see the silhouettes of five figures loitering about fifteen metres away. They weren't tall, and although Ricky couldn't see their faces, he knew they had to be Thrownaways.

Somewhere in the distance, a church bell struck twelve. Ricky put his hand in his pocket. The pen was there. He curled his fingers around it, then stepped forward, scanning the area ahead, his senses on high alert.

He took ten paces. The figures became clearer and he could make out the Thrownaways, their lean faces glowing yellow in the flickering street lamp. As they saw him approach, they congregated in a little group facing him. They did not look like a welcoming party. Ricky felt the scar on his wrist aching – his souvenir of his last encounter with kids like this. But suddenly Felix's training began to make sense. He no longer felt like the victim he had been when Felix had first found him.

He stopped walking when he was five metres

away from them. He gripped the pen more firmly, and realized that his palm was sweating.

One of the Thrownaways stepped forward. He was thin, with a scruffy mop of hair, a protruding Adam's apple and narrow, vicious eyes. His face looked like it had seen a few fists.

'You homeless?' Ricky said.

'Who's asking?'

A pause.

One of the other kids shouted out: 'What's the problem, Tommy?' But Tommy, if that was his name, didn't reply.

Ricky held out the rucksack.

'This is for you,' he said. 'Something to eat.'

Tommy looked at his friends. 'We've got a do-gooder,' he said, and his friends laughed unpleasantly.

Ricky remembered his own do-gooders, and he felt his lip curling.

'What else you got, do-gooder?' Tommy demanded. 'Empty out your pockets.'

Ricky threw the rucksack so that it landed halfway between him and the Thrownaways. 'Take it or leave it,' he said. He turned, and started walking back through the snow towards the main road.

There were footsteps behind him. He saw a shadow, cast by the flickering yellow street lamp, cross his own. He stopped and turned. Tommy was striding up to him, his fists clenched. 'I said, empty out your pockets!'

Ricky drew himself up to his full height, still clutching the pen in his pocket. Thanks to Felix's weeks of training, he felt strangely confident. 'There are two police officers just round the corner,' he said. 'You don't want to get mixed up with them any more than I do.'

The boy sneered, but Ricky immediately noticed the look of uncertainty in his eyes. 'Going to go off crying to the police?' Tommy asked.

'Not at all. But it'll be them taking you to A & E if you even think about attacking me. Take the food, share it with your friends. Think of this as your lucky night.'

There was clearly something in Ricky's voice that made him sound convincing. A flicker of hesitation crossed Tommy's face.

One of the other kids called out: 'Hunter's gonna want a wallet, innit?'

Tommy looked over his shoulder, but he didn't advance any further. He had clearly decided that Ricky wasn't easy pickings. 'You should get out of here, before we change our mind about you,' he muttered, then turned and walked back to his mates.

Ricky hurried back onto the main road. The

police were still there. The main road was still busy, the cars moving slowly through heavy snow. He hailed a cab, and went back home.

Madeleine would have approved, he told himself.

But he wondered what Felix would say.

If he told him . . .

10

THE PICTURE

In his past life, Boxing Day had always been a disappointment. It meant the excitement of Christmas was over. But when the doorbell rang at exactly 9 a.m. on the 26th, Ricky felt strangely relieved. His solitary Christmas was over. After all, there was only so much TV he could watch on his own, especially when it was all filled with images of families and parties. To stave off the boredom on Christmas Day, he'd even spent some time on the treadmill, but then felt sad that he was doing so on what was supposed to be a festive occasion. Still, at least he hadn't been dragged to that weird church by his foster carers . . . And now he could get back to work, if you wanted to call it that, with Felix.

But as soon as he opened the door to see his mentor standing there, his head and shoulders covered with a dusting of the snow that had not stopped falling since Christmas Eve, and with a storm cloud for a face, he could tell something was wrong.

Felix grunted an unfriendly greeting, then limped through the door and into the living room, leaving a trail of dirty snow behind him. He plonked himself down on the sofa. Ricky noticed that, unusually, he was carrying a small leather briefcase.

'Er, cup of tea?' Ricky offered. He wondered if Felix knew about his little excursion on Christmas Eve. Maybe he'd followed him, and Ricky hadn't noticed.

Felix shook his head curtly. He pulled a bag of sweets out of his pocket and was about to put one in his mouth. Before it touched his lips, he threw the sweet away at the coffee table. It pinged on the glass and ricocheted off like a bullet.

'Everything all right?' Ricky asked nervously.

'It's too early,' Felix said. 'You're not ready.'

Ricky frowned. 'Too early for what?'

'I *told* them. He's *good*, I said. *Very* good. A natural, even. But he's only covered basic observation, surveillance and improvised weaponry. He can't drive a vehicle or handle a gun. His navigation skills are elementary at best. He's never even jumped out of any aircraft, for pity's sake. He's just not ready to go out into the field. But would they listen? Would they . . . ?'

'What field?' Ricky interrupted him. At the mention of jumping out of an aircraft, he'd felt slightly sick. 'What are you *talking* about?'

Felix closed his eyes and drew a deep breath. Then he looked Ricky straight in the eye. 'Sit down, Coco,' he said.

'No. I want to know what's going on.'

'Then sit down, and I'll tell you.' Felix placed his briefcase on the coffee table and opened it up. 'For God's sake, Coco, just do as I say for once.'

Ricky sat.

Felix removed an iPad from inside his briefcase. He tapped the screen a couple of times and handed it to Ricky. 'Do you recognize this man?'

Ricky looked at the screen. A face looked back at him. It belonged to a man in a suit. He looked about fifty years old, with a tanned, handsome face and an insincere smile. Ricky didn't like the look of him, but he *did* recognize the face.

'Yeah,' he said.

'Where from?'

'I dunno. Telly, maybe.'

'He's the Right Honourable Jacob Cole. He used to be a businessman in the aerospace industry, now he's a Member of Parliament. Very influential man.

Highly respected. Has the Prime Minister's ear and some people think he might be PM himself one day.'

'Good for him.' Ricky tried to hand the iPad back, but Felix indicated that he should keep it.

'He has a daughter. Her name's Izzy. Fifteen years old. She's gone missing. Swipe the screen and you'll see a picture of her.'

Ricky swiped. As he looked at the screen, he felt his blood chill by several degrees. His muscles froze. He couldn't believe what he was seeing.

Madeleine.

He blinked, and stared. It took ten seconds for him to realize his mind was playing tricks on him. It wasn't Madeleine, of course, but the girl looked so like his sister that he couldn't stop staring at her. She was pretty, with the same blonde hair and the same piercing grey-green eyes, and she was smiling as if she hadn't a care in the world.

Ricky swallowed. This Izzy Cole was the spitting image of Madeleine. He looked up at Felix. Was this coincidence, or was his mentor playing some sort of mind game? Ricky wouldn't put it past him. 'Poor her,' he said carefully. 'But lots of kids go missing, right?'

If Felix was feeling sorry for the girl, he didn't look it. 'Jacob Cole wants his daughter back, naturally. He's been pulling strings.'

'Well, I'm guessing he's been pulling the wrong ones, if *we're* sitting here talking about it. Shouldn't the police be dealing with this?'

Felix narrowed his eyes and stared momentarily at Ricky. 'Swipe again,' he said.

Ricky swiped. He saw another picture. It was grainy and indistinct. Ricky could instantly tell that it was a still from a security camera, and he felt his body temperature lower a couple more degrees. He recognized the location as the busy road in King's Cross where he had been on Christmas Eve. He recognized Izzy Cole, looking a lot less pretty this time, her face bruised and her expression frightened. She was wearing a woollen hat, and his memory kicked in. Christmas Eve. She'd been by the main road . . . In the background, behind some drunks, he could just see another figure, his back to the camera, his head covered with a hood.

He looked up at Felix. Did his mentor know that it was Ricky himself there in the picture?

'That security camera spotted her over Christmas around King's Cross,' Felix said. 'We can't be sure if she's still there, but there's a high population of young homeless people in that area. It we're going to find her, that's the best place to start.'

'We?' Ricky said.

Felix looked uncomfortable. 'What I mean is:

you. There's very little chance that these homeless youngsters will speak to the police, or even to another adult. We've tried to engage with them before. They just close up. We need *you* to make contact. Find out if any of these homeless kids have seen Izzy. If so, where and when.'

Ricky put the iPad down on the table. 'What if I say I won't do it?'

Felix blinked. 'I told them you might say that. I told them you weren't ready. I told them they should call in Agent 21.'

Ricky felt the anger rising in him again. 'Why have you always got to talk in riddles? Who's Agent 21? Who are *they*?'

A pause.

'Agent 21,' Felix said finally, 'is like you. About the same age, a little older perhaps. Highly skilled, one of our best-kept secrets. "They" are a government agency. I work for them. Agent 21 works for them. So do you, now.'

'I don't work for *anyone*.'

'If you say so, Coco.' Suddenly Felix was maddeningly calm. He looked all around him. 'Pretty neat pad, this, for someone without a job.'

'What's it called, this agency?'

'I'm not going to tell you. It isn't important, anyway. Names are just . . . well, never mind.

What's important is that we – *you* – find Izzy Cole.'

'Why can't you just send in your precious Agent 21 if he's so great?'

'Because he doesn't know the streets like you. You're the better asset for the job. At least, that's what my superiors think. But they've been wrong before,' he added darkly.

Ricky stood up. He paced the room, fully aware that Felix was staring at him.

– Maybe now is the time to go? To take the money and run.

– But it's just one girl. We could try to find her. If we manage it, great. If not . . .

– But it's not our problem . . .

– She's probably rich. If we find her and bring her back to her family, there might be a reward in it for us.

Ricky turned to Felix. 'It's an impossible task,' he said. 'The girl could be anywhere. That picture was taken more than twenty-four hours ago.'

Felix gave him a sharp look. 'How do you know when it was taken?'

'You must have said.'

But they both knew he hadn't. Ricky felt himself blushing. He started talking to hide it. 'She could have travelled to, I don't know, Scotland in that time.'

'Unlikely,' Felix stated. 'Work like this is all about patterns. When people disappear, they normally don't move too far from their first destination. I'd bet money that she's still in London.'

'London's a big place.'

'Then you'd better get started, Coco.'

Ricky paused. His mind was working overtime. How would he do this? Where would he start? He remembered Tommy, the aggressive Thrownaway with the protruding Adam's apple he'd met on Christmas Eve. Maybe if Ricky could find him again, it would give him a lead on Izzy Cole. But he didn't like the idea.

'Those street kids. They don't talk to just anyone, you know. They have gangs. Some of them are violent.'

'Then you'd better be persuasive.'

'And if I can't be persuasive?'

Felix stared at him. 'Look at her face, Coco. She's in a bad way. You know yourself how dangerous it is for a kid to be living on the street. What would have happened to you in Bloomsbury Square if I hadn't shown up to help you out?' He got to his feet and limped over to where Ricky was standing. 'Not everybody has a guardian angel, kid. Are you going to let the streets destroy that girl, just because you're feeling too selfish to use everything I've taught you to help someone who needs it?'

Ricky clenched his jaw and stared fiercely into the middle distance.

– He's talking you into it. Ignore him. Don't let him get to you, Ziggy said in his head.

– But he's right. You saw what she looked like. She was a mess. Maybe I can help . . . And she's been beaten up. Like Madeleine was. What if she . . . wants to kill herself too? I couldn't save Madeleine, but maybe I can save this girl?

Ricky felt his mouth turn dry. He knew Felix was using him. But he also felt a twinge of excitement and realized he was up for the challenge. For some reason he didn't want Felix to see that.

'What do I do if I find her?' he asked.

'*When* you find her,' Felix replied, 'you bring her here and you call me.' From his pocket he removed a mobile phone. 'Speed dial one,' he said. 'There are no other numbers programmed on it. But you call immediately. Is that understood?'

'Yeah,' Ricky said. 'That's understood.' He took the phone, delighted to see it was an up-to-date model. If this all went belly-up, at least he could sell it . . .

Felix had gone. Ricky stood in his bedroom, a bad feeling about what he'd just agreed to do hanging over him like a cloud.

The wardrobe doors were open. He needed to choose his clothes carefully. He found that his mentor's words were echoing in his head. *When you're following someone, you need to make sure you pay attention to what you're wearing. Make sure it's appropriate to where you are. If you're in a rough, poor area, wearing all the latest designer gear will make you stick out like a sore thumb.*

He pulled out a pair of jeans. He'd worn them several times, but they still looked far too new. So he went to the kitchen and found a good, sharp knife, which he used to rip some holes in them. He then spent a good half an hour fraying the rips with his fingertips. He selected the same, slightly smelly, T-shirt he'd worn for the past few days, and a thin jumper into the elbows of which he tore more holes. Then he checked out the whole ensemble in the mirror. Not bad. He tousled his hair a little, and decided that at the very least he looked un-remarkable.

Felix had left him a printout of the photo of Izzy Cole, because brandishing an iPad on the dingier streets of London would be a sure way to get mugged. He folded it carefully and put it into his back pocket. He also pocketed the phone Felix had given him. With the press of a few buttons he brought up his own number, and found himself able to memorize it at a glance. Then he stuffed it into a front pocket of his jeans where no nimble fingers would be able to snatch it without his knowing. Then he left the flat.

Outside, the visibility was poor on account of the blizzard. There was more than thirty centimetres of snow piled up on one of the benches, but the ground was carpeted in unpleasant grey-brown slush. Ricky was cold through before he'd even walked twenty metres.

He had also noticed the figure tailing him. For some reason it made him angry that Felix, after all the surveillance training they'd done, should have someone following him in such an unskilled way. As he walked across the plaza, Ricky pretended not to notice. But all the while, his eyes scanned ahead and his brain worked overtime as he searched for a way to lose the tail. In the end, he decided to wait until he had ducked down into Canary Wharf underground station.

He sensed his tail following him down the escalators into the ticket office. They were ten metres behind as he swiped his Oyster card. And as he waited for his train, he could sense the figure standing on the platform, still about ten metres to his left. Ricky didn't look at him directly, but could tell that the tail was a man wearing jeans and a black raincoat, probably in his twenties.

A train arrived. Ricky stepped in. So did his pursuer. Ricky stood right by the doors.

An announcement came over the tube's loud-speaker. 'Stand clear of the doors please.'

A hissing sound from the doors themselves. They started to close. Quick and agile, Ricky slipped back through them and onto the platform. He considered winking at his tail to let him know he had noticed him. But he decided not to rub it in. He just turned his back on the train as it moved away, taking his pursuer with it. Then he headed along the brightly lit corridors of the underground station to find the platform he *really* wanted.

Ricky took the tube to King's Cross. He realized that finding a lone girl in London was like looking for a needle in a haystack, but that was definitely the best place to start looking. And if he couldn't find the girl, well, maybe the boy Tommy would be able to help . . .

Despite the Christmas sales, the snow seemed to have lessened the crowds, so the main road outside the station was not as busy as it had been on Christmas Eve. There were no police officers directing the traffic and Ricky's visibility through the snow was little more than five or six metres. He crossed the road and headed towards the side street where he'd had his encounter with the Thrownaways.

It looked empty. Snow had drifted heavily to one side. Several cars looked like they would have to wait for a thaw before they could move. With his shoulders hunched and his hands dug deep into his pockets, Ricky tramped up the pavement. He realized that his every sense was on high alert – in a way that it never had been before he met Felix. He heard a crow cawing from a rooftop on the opposite side of the street. The wind whistled as it gusted between the high buildings on either side. Ricky wiped his numb nose with the back of his sleeve, then noticed a passer-by walking in the opposite direction. Ricky didn't slow down, or even raise his head. But his eyes were fixed on the pedestrian. A woman. Heavy fur coat. A furry scarf that looked like she had an animal draped over her neck. Expensive clothing. Ricky caught a whiff of perfume, and looked over his shoulder to watch her disappear . . .

'Spare some change?'

Ricky started. The voice came from just a couple of metres away. He looked to his right to see a man curled up in a doorway, blowing into his hands to keep them warm. He had a grizzled face, cracked, bleeding lips and dark rings under his eyes. Ricky gave himself a silent telling-off for having missed him, but then shoved his hand into his pocket and brought out some change. He dropped the money in the snow on the edge of the pavement, and watched for a moment as the homeless man scrabbled around in the powder to find it. Once the man had collected all the coins, Ricky bent down to look him straight in the eye. 'You should get a hot drink,' he said.

The man looked at the change in his trembling hand. 'With fifty p?'

Ricky fished another handful of change from his pocket, but he didn't hand it over just yet. Instead, he removed the photograph of Izzy, unfolded it and waved it under the homeless man's nose. 'I'm looking for this girl. Have you see her?'

The homeless man stared at the picture for a few seconds. Then he shook his head. Ricky handed over his fistful of change, gave him a nod of thanks and continued walking a few metres up the street.

Suddenly he stopped. He turned round and tramped back to the man in the doorway.

'There's this kid I met round here, a couple of days ago. Dark hair, thin, big Adam's apple. You know him?'

'Maybe,' the homeless man wheezed.

'What's his name?'

The man made a suggestive shrug. Ricky took more money from his pocket – a ten-pound note this time. He held it out, but just as the man made to grab the money, he whipped it back. 'His name?' he said.

'Tommy. He works this area for . . .' The man hesitated.

'For who?'

'No one.'

Ricky pulled yet another note from his pocket and waved it in front of the man. 'For who?' he insisted.

The man's eyes narrowed. 'Hunter,' he breathed.

– *You've heard that name before. One of the Thrownaways used it on Christmas Eve. And the guy you met was definitely called Tommy.*

– *Maybe all that Kim's game stuff wasn't just a party trick.*

'Who's Hunter?'

The man licked his cracked lips. 'Give me the money.'

Ricky handed over the two notes. The man grabbed them greedily.

'*Who's Hunter?*'

'Someone you should stay clear of, kid.'

'Where do I find him?'

'He moves around, doesn't he? Never stays in one

place.' The homeless man hesitated. 'Do you know Keeper's House?'

Ricky shook his head.

'It's a derelict building off Berwick Street in Soho. Hunter's running his kids from there, last I heard.'

'What do you mean, running his kids?'

'They steal for him. Pickpocketing, break-ins, sometimes worse. Do yourself a favour, lad. Stay away from Hunter and his crowd. You don't want to get involved.'

— *A Fagin, then*, Ricky thought.

— *Like in the musical. But this is real life. I'm guessing there's no singing and dancing . . .*

He nodded and thanked the man, then walked back through the snow to Euston Road with the man's warning ringing in his head: *You don't want to get involved.*

Too late, he reminded himself. He already was.

11

KEEPER'S HOUSE

Ricky stood on the corner of Berwick Street and D'Arblay Street, and shivered. He felt like the cold winter air had seeped into his very bones.

He pulled the phone from his pocket and Googled Keeper's House. It looked just as the homeless man had described it: derelict. The picture he'd found on the internet showed a boarded-up, graffitied house. And according to the map on his phone, it was just fifty metres from where Ricky was standing. He walked along Berwick Street for about thirty seconds, then took a right into a small side street, followed by another left turn ten metres along.

The street that led to Keeper's House was little more than an alleyway in which the snow was piled thickly. The house itself was at the end of the street.

It looked forbidding and disused. Had there been no snow, Ricky would never have imagined it was occupied. But his eyes instantly picked out several trails of footprints in the snow along the street.

He heard Felix's voice in his mind. *You need to see everything.*

He zoned in on the footprints. They were all pointing away from Keeper's House and he reckoned he could make out five separate sets – that meant five people had left the house in the past few hours, and they'd not yet come back.

Decision time. Should Ricky break into Keeper's House and try to find the young homeless guy who'd called himself Tommy? Should he risk coming face to face with this Hunter character, whoever he was? Or should he wait here for the return of who-ever had left Keeper's House that day?

He decided to wait.

Ricky took up a position in a doorway just opposite the entrance to the side street. He was mostly protected from the snow here, but not from the cold. He crouched down, huddled into a ball, his head bowed but his eyes fixed on the entrance to the side street.

And he waited.

He was numb with cold within half an hour. After an hour, he could barely think straight. It occurred to him that the Ricky who had never met Felix would *never* have put himself through this. He was too cold even for his teeth to chatter.

– *Remind me again why we're doing this.*

– *Shut up, Ziggy.*

He kept watching.

They arrived after two hours. Ricky's feet had gone beyond feeling like blocks of ice. Now he couldn't feel them at all.

There were three of them. They had a dejected air as they tramped through the snow, their hands buried deep in their pockets for warmth. None of them noticed Ricky, huddled in his doorway. Ricky watched them carefully. He examined their clothes: old, threadbare. Glimpses of the side of their faces: wary, aggressive. Their gait: tired. He compared them to his memory of Tommy from Christmas Eve. None of them resembled him.

– *What do we do now, Sherlock? Approach them? Ask if any of them know—*

– *Wait! Who's that?*

Approaching from the opposite direction was a figure Ricky recognized. Lanky. Thin. A protruding Adam's apple and a scowl on his face.

Tommy.

He looked almost as cold as Ricky, with snow settling on his hunched shoulders. His lips had a faintly blue cast, and Ricky thought he could see a blood stain under his nose and over his upper lip. Last time Ricky had seen him, when they had faced up to each other in the side street by King's Cross two nights ago, he'd worn a mask of aggression. But now, when he didn't know he was being watched, Tommy looked like any other lost kid. Before meeting Felix, Ricky had felt slightly scared in the presence of one of these Thrownaways, but right now he just felt a bit sorry for him.

Even so, he remembered Felix's words: *You always want an escape route.* He glanced to both ends of the street. If it came to it, he could sprint in either direction . . .

'Tommy!'

The Thrownaway stopped in his tracks. At first it looked like he hadn't even seen Ricky. Then Ricky stood up slowly, Tommy peered at him, and a look of recognition slowly dawned on his face. Followed by a look of confusion.

'What do *you* want?' he said.

'I need your help.'

'Get out of here, if you know what's good for you.'

'I hope you enjoyed that food I gave you,' Ricky said. 'There's more where that came from.'

Tommy scowled. 'What do you think I am, some sort of charity case?'

– That was the wrong thing to say. You need to backtrack quickly.

'Course not. Look, the other night, I was looking for a girl. She's lost. I've got a picture here . . .' He held it out, the good picture, the one where Izzy looked blonde and pretty and not beaten up.

A missed beat. Tommy glanced down at the picture, then looked away momentarily.

– He's seen her. You can tell by looking at him. He doesn't want you to know.

'What's that got to do with me?'

– Flatter him. Use his ego.

'She was on your turf. I bet you know *everything* that goes on there.' Tommy shrugged modestly as Ricky added: 'You and Hunter.'

Tommy seemed to catch his breath. He looked at Ricky even more warily. 'How do you know Hunter?' He narrowed his eyes. 'If you're with the police . . .'

'I'm fourteen, Tommy. Bit young for a copper, don't you think?'

Tommy narrowed his eyes. 'Yeah,' he mumbled. 'Maybe.'

Ricky walked up to him and smiled his most reasonable smile. 'Where is she, mate?'

Tommy looked left and right – rather nervously, Ricky thought. 'You'd better speak to Hunter,' he said. He pointed towards Keeper's House. 'It's this way.'

They trudged through the snow. Ricky sensed that Tommy wanted to say something, but was holding back. He tried to draw him into conversation.

'What happened to your nose? Looks like you've been bleeding.'

Tommy seemed embarrassed. 'Tried to snatch a bag,' he said. 'The woman chased me. I slipped in the snow and hurt myself.'

'Blow out,' Ricky said, and they tramped on in silence.

Only when they were at the front entrance to Keeper's House – a big arched door covered with graffiti tags – did Tommy speak again.

'If you want something from Hunter,' he said, 'you have to give *him* something in return. And don't try to mess with him, because then he'll mess with you, twice as hard.'

Ricky nodded. 'Got it,' he said.

– But what have you got to give him?

– We'll think of something.

Tommy opened the door and led Ricky into a grubby hallway with peeling wallpaper and a damp atmosphere. It was barely any warmer in here than outside. To the left was a door, slightly ajar. Ricky followed Tommy through it and down a dark flight of stone steps. They led into a large, dimly lit basement room with items of shabby furniture dotted around. Ricky's eyes picked out the three Thrownaways he'd seen approaching Keeper's House, huddled on sofas and armchairs along with another six youngsters. They were all eyeing him carefully as he entered.

But none of them were eyeing him so carefully as the man who emerged from the shadows in a far corner of the room. He looked about sixty, with a nose that had been broken more than once and greedy, watery eyes that were full of suspicion.

'Empty-handed again, Tommy?' the old man rasped. 'You ain't paying your way, son.'

Tommy bowed his head.

'But it looks like you brought old Hunter a guest. Is that right?'

Tommy didn't reply and Ricky could tell he was frightened. Everyone in this gloomy basement was frightened. Including Ricky.

He stepped forward. 'I need some help,' he said.

A nasty smile spread across Hunter's face. 'Did you hear that?' he announced to the room in general. 'Our young friend here needs some help.' He stepped up to Ricky, face to face with him, close enough for Ricky to smell his foul breath. 'Trouble is, sunshine, that we're not in the business of helping strangers. In fact, and here's the funny thing . . .' With this, he looked round to the others in the room with an even broader, more loathsome smile. 'The funny thing is, we do exactly the opposite, don't we, lads?'

There was a muttering of agreement around the room. Ricky glanced over at Tommy, who subtly mouthed the words: '*Get out!*'

Too late.

For a man in his sixties, Hunter moved fast. He thrust out his right hand and grabbed Ricky by the throat, squeezing hard as he pushed him up against the wall. Ricky felt his whole body jar with the impact as Hunter whispered: 'You shouldn't have come here, sunshine.'

Ricky could barely breathe, let alone speak clearly. His throat burned as he tried to talk. 'I . . . I've got something for you,' he whispered.

Hunter sneered. 'Oh, yeah? What are you then, Father bleedin' Christmas?'

'S – seriously, I've got something . . .'

Hunter gave a barking laugh. 'So what is it, sunshine? What's this amazing gift of yours?'

Ricky struggled for breath as he answered: 'Your wallet.'

Silence in the room. Hunter's watery eyes narrowed again. Slowly he released his grip on

Ricky's throat and Ricky inhaled deeply as Hunter patted down his own pockets. When he couldn't find what he was looking for, Ricky held up the heavy black wallet that he had taken from Hunter's overcoat just minutes before the old man had grabbed his throat.

It was as if the whole room was holding its breath, waiting to see how Hunter would react. Ricky handed him the wallet, which Hunter snatched back. Then Ricky removed the photograph of Izzy Cole from his back pocket again and held it up. 'I'm looking for this girl,' he said. 'I think you might know where she is.' He examined Hunter's face as he said this. There was a flicker of recognition. Hunter knew who Izzy Cole was – Ricky was sure of it.

'What if I do?' Hunter said, his voice dangerous.

'Here's what I think,' Ricky replied. He looked around the room. All eyes were on him. 'You send the boys and girls in this room out to rob for you. In return, you give them a place to stay and food to eat so they don't have to live on the street.' Ricky sniffed, then looked directly at Hunter again. 'I'm the best pickpocket you ever met,' he said. 'I'll teach Tommy how to do it. He can teach the others. In return, you let me talk to the girl.'

Hunter's face was expressionless. He turned his

back on Ricky and paced for twenty seconds, examining the wallet in his hand.

Suddenly he spun round. 'If I find out you're a copper—' he started to say.

'He's only fourteen, Hunter!' Tommy cut in, using Ricky's own words. 'Course he's not a copper.'

Hunter stared at Ricky again, as though sizing him up. 'All right,' he breathed. 'Take Tommy out now. If you come back with enough cash, maybe we can help. Tommy and the boys see things when they're out and about – right, lads?' There was a murmured agreement as Hunter strode up to Ricky, face to face again. 'And if you come back with nothing, I wouldn't bother showing your face round here again. Do you get my drift?'

'Yeah,' Ricky said quietly. 'I get your drift.'

12

MAGIC TRICKS

'Hunter's a piece of work, eh?' Ricky said to Tommy as they trudged through the snow away from Keeper's House. 'Why do you and the others stick around with him?'

'You wouldn't understand,' Tommy said. He was still scowling.

'Try me.'

Tommy gave him a sidelong glance, then shrugged. 'All right. Most of us have run away from home. We look like kids – we *are* kids. If anyone finds us sleeping rough, we get picked up by the police and sent back where we came from. None of us wants that, and Hunter knows it. He finds places for us to hide – places like Keeper's House. As long as we keep stealing for him, he lets us stay.'

'And if you don't?'

'He kicks us out.'

'What a gent.' They turned onto Brewer Street and started walking south.

'It's better than the alternative,' Tommy said.

Ricky remembered the seedy room he'd rented from Baxter. A horrible place, but he'd been grateful for it. 'I think I know what you mean,' he said.

'Whatever.' Tommy obviously didn't want to talk about it.

'Do you know where that girl is?' Ricky asked. He looked straight ahead as he put the question. But there was meaning in his voice. They both knew what could happen on the streets to runaway girls.

Tommy didn't answer and Ricky could sense something. Fear? Was Tommy scared of what Hunter would do if he gave up that information? Probably, Ricky decided. He decided not to push it. His best strategy was to gain Tommy's trust.

They walked on in silence for a couple of minutes, before Tommy glanced sideways at Ricky. 'So,' he said, 'what's your big pickpocketing secret?'

Ricky took a moment to order his thoughts. This was something he knew a lot about, from his months on the street. 'Have you ever seen a magic trick?' he asked.

'Yeah,' Tommy said. 'Course.'

'Well, here's what nobody ever tells you. Every

magic trick is the same. They're all about distraction. The magician gets you to think about something else while he performs the actual trick. Nine times out of ten, he knows what your card is, or which hat the bunny's in, right from the very start of the trick. The rest of it is all misdirection.'

'What's that got to do with stealing?'

'Everything. Picking a pocket is just the same as doing a magic trick. It's misdirection. If you manage to distract your mark, the job's done. You can pick their pocket all day long.' Ricky could tell he had Tommy's interest. 'Of course,' he continued, 'sometimes you don't even have to distract them. Sometimes they do it for you.'

'What do you mean?'

'You want to know the easiest place to pick a pocket?'

'Where?'

'Heathrow, Terminal Two. There's always delays. When there is, people find somewhere to sit and spread their stuff all over the place, including their hand luggage. Then they have their nose in a book or a newspaper. It's crazy – you can just stick your hand inside their luggage and grab their wallets. They normally have plenty of cash too, because they're going on holiday.'

They were on Shaftesbury Avenue now. There

were more people around, mostly heading towards
Piccadilly tube station, huddled against the snow,
their arms filled with Christmas sales shopping.

'Where else?' Tommy asked. Some of the
surliness had left his voice.

'Near the universities is good, especially in the
summertime. The students head off to the local
parks to read and work. They're just like the holiday-
makers. They spread out their stuff and don't pay
much attention to it. You can pretty much help
yourself.' He looked up at the sky meaningfully.
'Not much chance of that in this weather, though.
Day like this, you have to do some distraction.'

– *You realize you're beginning to sound like Felix.*

– *Maybe that's not such a bad thing. He's a good
teacher . . .*

'Let's head down into the tube station,' Ricky
said. 'I want to show you something.'

Piccadilly Circus underground was teeming with
people. The floors were damp with slush, and lots of
the pedestrians were carrying shopping bags from
the sales in nearby Regent Street and Oxford Street.
Ricky and Tommy stood by a tube map, their backs
against the walls. Just next to them was a poster
which said: 'Pickpockets are operating in this area.'
Ricky's eyes instantly picked out two London
Underground staff chatting to each other fifteen

metres to his two o'clock. Other than that, he saw nobody else in uniform.

'So,' Ricky said, just loud enough for Tommy to hear him above the hubbub. 'How do we tell where people are keeping their wallets?'

Tommy gave him a blank look. 'I dunno,' he said. 'Look for a bulge in their pockets, I suppose.'

'That's one way,' Ricky said. 'But I've got a better one. Watch carefully.' He stepped forward a couple of paces, then feigned a panicked expression and started patting himself down. 'Someone's stolen my wallet!' he called out – not so loud that the whole station would hear, but loud enough for everyone within four or five metres to register what he'd said. That meant about twenty people.

Nearly all of them did the same thing when they heard Ricky: their hands immediately went to one or other of their pockets, or to their shoulder bags or handbags. Within a couple of seconds, they had revealed to Ricky the location of their valuables.

Tommy was standing next to him again. 'Did you see that?' Ricky breathed.

'Yeah,' Tommy said. There was a hint of admiration in his voice. 'Nice.'

Ricky was in the zone. And there was something else. He'd been a good pickpocket before. But now, thanks to Felix's training, he felt even more confident. He was alert. Aware of everything around him. He reckoned there wasn't a single person in this train station he couldn't steal from.

For now, he had his eyes on a slim man with short brown hair. This man had touched the rear right-hand pocket of his jeans, so Ricky knew that was where he kept his money. 'Walk behind me,' he told Tommy. 'Get ready to take a wallet if I give it to you.'

Ricky followed his mark closely as he walked straight up to the ticket barriers, feeling dry-mouthed with excitement. It felt good to be doing this again. As the man stood in front of the barriers and slapped his Oyster card onto the sensor, Ricky purposefully barged into the back of him. The man looked round, clearly very irritated.

'I'm *really* sorry,' said Ricky. 'That was *so* clumsy of me.' His apology seemed to calm the man down. He turned back round to face the barrier, which was now wide open. As he stepped forward, Ricky skilfully picked the wallet from his back pocket. He passed it back to Tommy as the man passed through the barrier, which slid shut.

'Back up,' Ricky hissed. He and Tommy stepped away from the barrier and back into the crowd. After a couple of seconds, they turned to watch their mark. He was standing at the top of the escalators, patting himself down, just like Ricky had pretended to do.

'He knows he's been done,' said Tommy.

'Yeah,' Ricky replied. The man looked panicked. You could see it in his face and his body language.

Then, for the first time ever, Ricky felt a pang. He remembered something Felix had said. *Oh, you never know, Coco. One day you might surprise yourself.*

– *Guilt, Ricky?*

– *Maybe, a little.*

– *Would it help to remember that you're doing this for a reason. You're trying to help Izzy Cole, remember.*

He turned to Tommy. 'I call that technique the turnstile jam. I don't *think* our mark felt me take his wallet, but it wouldn't really matter if he did. Look, *he's* stuck on the other side of the barriers and *we're* hidden in the crowd. Did you see how I distracted him by bumping into the back of him?'

'Not very subtle,' Tommy said.

'Course not,' Ricky replied. 'If it was subtle, it wouldn't be a distraction. Come on, let's get back up to the street. I've got a few more tricks to show you.'

And he did. Over the next two hours, Ricky showed Tommy how to perfect the Fake Lift. ('One of us makes a clumsy attempt at picking someone's pocket. They realize someone's trying to rob them and make a big fuss. When their guard's down, the

second person goes in and *actually* lifts the wallet.')
He talked him through the 'Guess Who' trick.
('I run up behind the mark, put my hands over their
eyes and shout "Guess who!" When they turn
round, I act all embarrassed and explain that I
mistook them for my mum or dad. While they're
distracted by apology, you go in for the kill.) He
taught Tommy about the pickpocket's most useful
tool. ('A razor blade, good and sharp. You make a slit
under the mark's pocket and the wallet just falls
out.') He even shared the old 'clumsy trip' trick that
he'd pulled on Felix all those weeks ago. ('Good one
for us kids, that. Appeals to the mark's better nature.
And, er . . . if you can smear a bit of blood on your
knee or elbow it works even better . . .')

By the end of the afternoon, they had quite a
haul. Five wallets, and well over £300 in cash. And
in one of the wallets, there was a unexpected bonus.
Inside the pouch meant for coins there was a gold
ring with a small gemstone set into it.

'Might be diamond,' Tommy said in an awed
voice.

Ricky shrugged. 'Maybe,' he said. He gave it to
Tommy. 'No need to tell Hunter about that, eh?'

Tommy took the ring with trembling hands.
'There's this guy in Chancery Lane,' he said. 'I think
he's called Randolph – at least, that's the name over

his shop. He's a fence – you know, someone who'll buy any stolen goods. I've heard people say he pays good money for jewellery, no questions asked . . .'

Tommy's eyes shone with the thrill of it. But not Ricky's. Each time he had watched their mark walk away, unsuspectingly poorer, he felt more deflated. He knew that his skills were good, but was this *really* how he wanted to spend his time?

Wasn't he a better person than this? Hadn't his life improved since he'd stopped relying on petty crime?

The light was failing, and the snow had started to fall heavily again. 'Let's get back to Keeper's House,' he suggested. He immediately sensed Tommy's spirits fall, but he reminded himself that he had a job to do, and that job was to find Izzy Cole.

The gloomy basement was no different from how they'd left it. Hunter's Thrownaways were still lounging around the old furniture, and it was still cold. Hunter was creeping around in the shadows, like a spider patrolling its lair. When Ricky and Tommy appeared, he scuttled forward, his watery eyes suddenly bright and greedy.

'Well?' he demanded of Tommy.

Tommy opened up his shoulder bag and presented Hunter with the five wallets. The older man immediately started riffling through them, pulling out the cash and disregarding the credit cards. He counted the notes precisely, licking his forefinger every time he peeled one off. When he'd finished, he looked sharply at Tommy. 'Did you take any of the cash for yourself?' he demanded.

Tommy shook his head, a bit nervously.

Ricky decided he needed to change the subject. He stepped forward. 'Time to keep your end of the bargain, Hunter. Where do I find the girl?'

Hunter stepped forward, a nasty grin on his face. 'Quite the pushy little fella, aren't we?' he rasped. 'Well, maybe I don't *feel* like keeping my end of the bargain. Did you think about that?'

Ricky stayed very calm. 'Of course I thought about that,' he replied. 'Would you like to know what I decided?'

'I can hardly wait,' Hunter whispered nastily.

– You'd better come up with something good, Ricky. Hunter isn't the kind to play games.

But Ricky was making this up as he went along. As he spoke, he remained aware of the entrance to the basement in the corner of his eye. *Always have an escape route.*

– He's greedy. Greedy people all have the same weakness.

'I decided that you're a businessman. I'm going to need a place to lie low from time to time. Keeper's House would suit me just right. Every time I turn up, I'll bring you a few full wallets. Think of me as a regular income.'

Hunter and Ricky locked gazes. Thirty seconds passed. Hunter said nothing. He was clearly unsure whether to trust Ricky.

It was time to gamble.

'Fine,' Ricky announced. He nodded at Tommy. 'Nice working with you, buddy,' he said. Then he turned and headed back to the staircase.

'Wait!'

Hunter's voice was hoarse. Ricky turned to see his face contorted.

'All right,' Hunter said. He looked at Tommy. 'Take him to her,' he said.

Tommy nodded. 'This way,' he told Ricky. And to Ricky's surprise, rather than lead him back up the stairs, he walked across the basement room towards the door on the far side.

– She was here all along?

– Either that or it's a trap. Maybe Hunter's trying to get you somewhere you can't escape.

Ricky didn't move. When Tommy was halfway across the basement, he looked back over his shoulder. 'Come on, then,' he said.

For the second time that day, Ricky felt the eyes of everyone in the basement on him.

'Bring her here,' he said quietly.

Nobody moved. Hunter's watery eyes grew narrow again.

Silence.

'Suspicious, ain't ya, fella?' Hunter said.

'I wonder why,' Ricky replied. Every cell in his body was screaming at him to get out of there.

Hunter looked over at Tommy. Then he nodded. Tommy continued his walk across the basement. When he reached the door, he hesitated for a moment, then opened it and entered the adjoining room.

Thirty seconds passed.

A minute.

Hunter didn't take his eyes off Ricky. Nor did any of the other Thrownaways. He felt the scar on his wrist start to tingle.

— *We should get out of here. Something's wrong.*

— *Wait! I can hear movement . . .*

It came from the direction of the adjoining room. The door opened again and Tommy stepped out into the main basement room. Behind him, framed in the doorway, was the figure of a girl.

Ricky peered through the gloom to make out her features. He saw long hair, straggly, matted, dirty. Bloodshot eyes with huge black rings underneath them. Cracked lips. A frightened, pale face.

She didn't smile and she didn't move. But she

didn't have to. Ricky recognized her features. They were almost identical to those of his dead sister.

But this wasn't Madeleine.

Ricky had found Izzy Cole.

13

TRIDENT

Hunter sidled up to Ricky. 'She ain't leaving Keeper's House.'

'What if she wants to?'

Hunter gave him one of his nasty leers. 'Izzy, love,' he called across the basement to the girl. 'This fella wants a chat. Feel like going for a little walk with him?'

Izzy Cole shook her head. 'I'm not going anywhere,' she whispered. Her voice was cracked and weak, and her eyes darted around the room.

'Like I say' – Hunter smirked – 'she ain't leaving.'

Ricky stepped forward. His footsteps were the only noise in that basement. 'I just wanted to talk to you, Izzy. Is that all right?'

She looked uncertain. But after a few seconds, she nodded and disappeared back into the side room.

'You've got ten minutes,' Hunter muttered. 'Then I'm kicking you out.'

The side room was smaller than the main basement room. About ten metres by ten. The only light came from a bare bulb hanging from the ceiling. The floor was covered with thin, dirty mattresses. Clearly this was where the Hunter's Thrownaways slept. Izzy was in the far corner, huddled on the ground, clutching her knees. She stared, not at Ricky but into the middle distance, with big, lonely, frightened eyes.

'My name's Ricky.' He tried to sound friendly and upbeat. It was difficult in a place like this.

No reply.

'I'm here to help you.'

'I don't need any help,' Izzy said.

'I'm sorry, but . . . Ricky looked around meaningfully. 'It doesn't look like it.'

'You don't know what you're talking about,' Izzy whispered.

Ricky walked over and crouched down next to her. 'Your mum and dad want you back home,' he said.

Izzy gave a mirthless laugh. 'That's what they said, is it? Well, I'm not going. What's it got to do with you, anyway?'

Ricky didn't reply.

Izzy moved her head slightly to look at him. 'I think I've seen you before,' she said slowly.

Ricky nodded. 'Christmas Eve maybe? If you were around King's Cross then? In a woolly hat, right? I saw a picture of you there too. Your face was badly bruised. It looks a bit better now.'

Izzy touched her cheek. 'That's why I'm not going back,' she whispered. 'Who are you anyway? Did my dad send you?'

'No.'

'Then who did?'

A difficult question to answer. Ricky decided not to. 'Why don't you want to go home?' he asked.

'You wouldn't understand.'

Ricky stood up. He started pacing. 'I ran away from home too,' he said. 'Eighteen months ago. Never been back.'

He could instantly tell that he had Izzy's attention. 'Why?'

'I was living with foster parents. My mum and dad had died. My foster parents kept dragging me to this obscure church and saying he wanted to save my soul. Not a normal everyday church either, but some weird sect . . .'

'At least they didn't beat you up,' Izzy said. 'My dad just . . .' She touched her cheek again. '*Please* don't tell him where I am.'

Ricky looked towards the door. 'Why are you staying with Hunter, though?' he asked.

'I've got nowhere else. And I met Tommy and some of the others on the street and they said this was safer than being on my own . . .'

'I bet they did,' Ricky muttered. 'You know what he does? Hunter, I mean. You know that he gets these kids to steal for him?'

Izzy nodded. 'But,' she said quietly, 'he said I could just stay, and not do any of that.'

Ricky raised his eyebrow at her, but Izzy already seemed to know how naive she sounded.

'Are you going to tell my dad where I am?' she asked.

Ricky hesitated. He pulled his phone from his pocket. *Speed dial one. And you call immediately.* He took hold of Izzy's hand and wrote his number on the back of it. 'Hunter's bad news,' he said. 'Any time you need some help, just call.'

He walked towards the door.

'You haven't answered my question,' Izzy called after him. 'Are you going to tell my dad?'

Ricky paused and looked over his shoulder. 'Of course I'm not,' he said.

Eight p.m.

The first thing Ricky did when he was back at his

apartment was wash. Hot, steaming water that drove away the cold that had seeped into his bones, and cleaned off the grime and stench of Keeper's House. Only when he was out of the shower, dried and dressed, did he call Felix.

'I found her.'

There was a pause on the line.

'That was very quick, Coco.' Felix sounded genuinely surprised. 'Where is she?'

'I'm not going to tell you.'

He hung up.

Ricky reckoned it would be less than half an hour before Felix turned up at his door. He was right. Twenty-three minutes later the buzzer sounded. Ricky opened up and stepped aside as Felix limped into the apartment and through to the main room.

'What do you mean, you're not going to tell me?' Felix's face was unusually fierce.

'Which bit didn't you understand?' Ricky said.

Felix narrowed his eyes and peered at him. 'This isn't a game, Coco. It's serious.'

'And so am I. She ran away from home for a reason. Her dad was beating her up. I'm not going to let you send her back.'

'You don't know what you're talking about, Coco.'

'*No!*' Ricky blazed. '*You* don't know what you're

talking about. You've got no idea what it's like, being beaten up by someone older than you, day after day . . . It's what happened to my *sister*—'

Suddenly Ricky cut himself short. Felix had hitched up his trouser leg, just a few centimetres, to reveal the bottom of his prosthetic leg. Ricky stared at the narrow metal poles joining Felix's ankle to his knee, and suddenly felt rather ashamed of what he'd just said.

Felix let the trouser leg fall again. 'Sit down, Coco,' he said. 'Sit down, shut up, and listen.'

Ricky perched on the edge of the sofa. Felix sat opposite him.

'It's time you started to realize that the world really *is* more complicated than you thought. *Please*, Coco, just be quiet and don't answer back for once. Now, do you really think you can live in this kind of luxury, and receive the kind of education I've been giving you, and not have to give anything back?'

Ricky didn't reply.

'I've already told you this once. I work for a top-secret government agency. And as long as you live in this flat and receive weekly money and training, so do you. *Don't talk, Coco. Just listen!*'

Felix breathed deeply. He was clearly angry and trying to calm himself down. Ricky felt a strange chill – he suspected he wasn't going to like what he was about to hear.

'Part of our work is to recruit youngsters like you. Not just anyone, mind. They need to be bright and promising. They need to have skills a little out of the ordinary. And they need to be youngsters whose absence nobody would notice, or at least mind. It's a very precise profile, Coco, and you fit it. I'm good at spotting these youngsters, drawing them to me for the initial contact – remember what a mark I looked when you first saw me? – and you've already shown me time and again since then that you have a very high degree of aptitude for the work involved. Your *attitude* is a different matter, of course, but we can work on that.

'Now you're probably wondering why this agency needs to recruit young people. Well, certain situations sometimes arise where the presence of adult agents would be noticed. In these instances, we need to rely on kids. If you stop and think about it for a moment, none of this should come as too much of a surprise to you. And if you give it a moment's more thought, you should work out that we don't use this precious resource simply to hunt down runaway kids like Izzy Cole. Not unless there's a very good reason to do so.'

'So why are you so interested in her?' Ricky

asked. He spoke very quietly as he realized that there was more important stuff going on here than he could ever have imagined.

'I'm not interested in her,' Felix said. He sounded rather harsh. 'Not in the least. But I'm extremely interested in her father.'

'Because he beat her up?'

Felix gave Ricky a thin smile. 'No,' he said. 'Not because of that.' He stood up and started to pace. His limp seemed more pronounced than usual, and Ricky wondered if it hurt. Now wasn't the time to ask. Felix started to speak again. 'Does the word "Trident" mean anything to you?'

'I've heard it.'

'Do you know what Trident is?'

'Not really.' He wanted to add: 'I'm only fourteen, remember?' But he figured it wouldn't go down too well.

'Then listen hard, Coco. Trident is the United Kingdom's nuclear capability. It consists of four nuclear submarines each armed with D-5 ballistic missiles.'

At the word 'nuclear', Ricky felt faintly sick. 'What's a D-5 ballistic missile?' he asked.

Felix gave him a fierce stare. 'A big one,' he said. 'Each submarine contains forty thermonuclear warheads. At least one submarine is constantly in service around British waters. It's ready to launch a missile within a range of four thousand nautical miles, if the UK is provoked.'

Ricky felt a chill. 'Would that ever happen?' he asked.

'Nobody wants it to. It's called a nuclear deterrent. The idea is that as long as we have nuclear weapons, nobody will attack us, and as long as our enemies have them, we won't attack either. It works, because only a madman would want to start an all-out nuclear war.' Felix gave Ricky a piercing stare. 'Look out the window, Coco,' he said. 'Tell me what you see.'

Ricky walked up to the window and looked out over London. It was dark now, and the air was still thick with snow. It swirled in great torrents, and deadened the glow of the city lights. 'Snow,' he said. 'All I can see is snow.'

'Have you ever heard the phrase "nuclear winter"?'

Ricky shook his head. He didn't quite trust himself to speak.

'It's what scientists think will happen in the event of a major nuclear incident. The air gets filled with radioactive dust, the sun's rays get blocked out and the temperature on the ground lowers dramatically. We experience major climate change. You think the snow's bad tonight, Coco? Imagine what it's like during a nuclear winter – if you're lucky enough to survive the blast, that is, and you don't have radiation sickness eating into your body.'

'I get the point,' Ricky said quietly.

'Oh, *good*,' Felix said, his voice dripping with sarcasm. 'I *am* glad about that. So sit down again, and I'll tell you what all this has to do with Izzy Cole.'

Ricky returned to the sofa. He definitely felt sick now.

'The precise location of any given nuclear submarine is highly sensitive and secret information. If that information were to get into the wrong hands, there could be terrible repercussions.'

Ricky frowned. 'But you said yourself that only a madman would want to cause a nuclear war.'

'You're right. Unfortunately, such men exist. There are terrorists, or members of rogue states, who would pay a great deal of money for nuclear submarine location codes. And they would only pay such sums if they were prepared to use the information.'

Felix allowed that thought to sink in before continuing.

'We believe that Jacob Cole MP, Izzy's dad, has got his hands on these codes and is preparing to sell them to the highest bidder. Our sources suggest that they are probably Russian, but we don't know anything else about them.'

Ricky blinked.

'You look surprised, Coco. Don't be. You're pretty relaxed about stealing other people's belongings, but I like to think you have *some* sort of moral code. However, you'll soon learn that *some* people will do *anything* for money.'

'Can't they just change the codes?' Ricky asked.

'Of course. And as soon as they do, Cole will know.'

'Then why not, just, I don't know . . . sack him or something.'

'And let Cole's paymasters move on to somebody else who we have no intelligence on? Thanks, but no thanks. In any case, Cole is extremely close to the Prime Minister. The PM will never believe that he's guilty of such a crime.' He shook his head. 'Some issues are far too important to take to mere politicians. We have to deal with them discreetly ourselves. And that's why I need to get my hands on Izzy Cole. We've known for some time that her father has been violent to her. We know how much she hates him. That's why she's useful to us. We have a bucketload of rumour and hearsay about Jacob Cole, but we have no hard evidence, and that's what we *have* to get our hands on if we're going to bring him to justice. We need his daughter to *spy* on him. To gather information that will help us prove what he's up to. And to get our hands on the men he's in contact with.' He drew a deep, calming breath. 'It was extremely inconvenient for us when Izzy decided to run away from home. And that's why I need you to bring her to me. It's urgent, Ricky. More urgent than you can possibly know.'

Felix sat back and opened his arms in a gesture that said: *Over to you.*

Ricky paced. He felt Felix's eyes on him. He was confused. In the course of the past few minutes, life had turned serious. Half of him wondered if this was all some bad-taste joke. But then he looked around him again, at the plush, hi-tech surroundings in which he found himself. It was true. Nobody would pluck him from poverty and give him this sort of lifestyle without expecting something in return.

He trusted Felix. He *believed* him. His head swam with thoughts of submarines and nuclear winters. He didn't doubt that Felix was telling him the truth. He walked over to the window again, and stared out at the unwelcoming, threatening snow.

Then he turned.

'No,' he said.

Silence.

'Would you like to explain why?' Felix asked, his voice quiet and steady.

'You said you'd like to think I've got some sort of moral code. Well, here it is. My older sister killed herself because her foster parents were violent towards her. *Killed* herself, Felix. She wasn't much older than Izzy Cole.'

Ricky was determined not to let the tears come. He stared fiercely at Felix.

'It's not OK to send Izzy Cole back into a house where she's going to be beaten up. I saw the picture of her. It was bad.'

'But the *codes*, Coco.'

'That's a grown-ups' problem. You need to find a grown-ups' solution, not just enlist a bunch of kids to do your dirty work. Or maybe you can ask big bad Agent 21, if you can persuade him that it's OK for an adult to slap a kid around.' He looked at the room again. Sure, it was swish. Warm. Comfortable. But he'd lived without it before, and he could live without it again. 'I'm done with all this,' he said, and he walked out of the room.

He stormed into his bedroom, stuck his hand under his mattress and grabbed the sock where he had been carefully stashing his weekly money. It was empty. Ricky hurled it across the room. He didn't know how or when it had been emptied, but it just made him more angry. More determined to leave. He still had a bit of money in his trouser pocket – a few notes and a handful of change. That would have to be enough.

On his bedside table he noticed the snap gun Felix had given him on his first day, and which he'd gradually mastered over his time here. Could be useful, for a thief. He chucked it in a rucksack, then pulled on a thick jumper and coat. He grabbed a Nike baseball cap and put it on, the peak pointing backwards.

– *Are you sure you know what you're doing?*

– *Yep. It's over. I don't want to be part of this any more.*

He returned to where Felix was still sitting in the main room.

'You can't bring your sister back by saving Izzy Cole, you know,' Felix said quietly.

Ricky felt like spitting. 'Nice knowing you,' he said. 'Don't bother sending anyone to follow me this time. You know I'll only lose them.'

Felix didn't reply, so Ricky turned his back on him and left the flat, slamming the door behind him.

PART THREE

PART THREE

14

IZZY'S ESCAPE

Boxing Day, 11:30 p.m.

More than ever before, Ricky felt the need to be aware of people following him as he stormed out of the apartment block. He wasn't even subtle about checking for tails this time – he didn't have the patience any more. He just stopped every ten paces and looked around. Rather to his surprise, he didn't see anyone suspicious. A tall young woman with white-blonde hair cast him a sidelong glance as she walked past him, but moments later she had disappeared round a corner and Ricky noticed nobody else who looked even remotely out of the ordinary.

Maybe Felix really was just letting him go.

The night was bitterly cold so he couldn't stay on the streets. He needed somewhere to spend the night. But where?

– You could always go back to the apartment if you've quite finished with your little tantrum.

– No way. Me and Felix are finished.

He saw a cab coming from the opposite direction. Its orange 'For Hire' light was on. Ricky started to raise his hand to flag it down, but then he lowered it, aware that he had very little money now. He turned his baseball cap so the peak was pointing forward, then hurried over to the underground station. Down by the ticket barriers, he was about to swipe his Oyster card when he stopped himself again. Could Felix, or the strange, shadowy people he worked for, track him using the Oyster card? It wouldn't surprise him.

He bought himself a ticket instead, and took a train into Piccadilly Circus. Then he walked through the back streets of Soho – a stone's throw from Keeper's House – until he came to a busy little coffee shop on Frith Street that he knew was open all night. For the price of a few hot drinks, he could stay here till dawn.

He took a seat by the steamed-up window and ordered a hot chocolate, which he sipped slowly. There was a free newspaper at his table, which he pretended to read. In reality, his mind was churning over what he'd learned during the past couple of hours. Jacob Cole, MP. Nuclear submarines. These sounded like things that belonged to somebody else's life, not his. Why should he have to worry about them?

— *You're being childish.*

— *Well, get over it. I am a child.*

— *And how long are you going to use that as an excuse for doing nothing with your life? What do you want to be, the oldest pickpocket in town?*

— *Shut up, Ziggy.*

The voice in his head fell silent and Ricky sipped at his coffee. He looked around the café at the other customers. They were a mixed bunch: a few young couples; a little group of teenagers. An older man in the corner nursing a small espresso. A boy about Ricky's age, maybe a little older, with a red baseball cap worn backwards, sat at a table with a blond-haired man with a serious face. His older brother maybe? None of them paid Ricky any attention. Ricky realized his brain was in record mode, just like Felix had told him it must always be.

The door opened. An old lady shuffled in. She was probably in her seventies, wore tatty clothing and carried a full plastic bag close to her chest. She sat down at the table next to Ricky and started counting out a few coins in her grubby hands. When she was sure she had enough, she flagged down the waiter. Ricky felt sorry for her. He was sure she wouldn't have enough money to stay here till dawn, and he wondered where she would end up spending the night.

– *Maybe you're not quite as heartless as I thought.*

– *What are you talking about? I'm not heartless.*

– *Really? Could have fooled me. You seem quite happy to leave people to die.*

– *Don't be stupid, Ziggy. I've never left anybody to die.*

– *Oh, really? And what happens if the wrong people get hold of the codes for those nuclear submarines? Who do you think comes off worse in the disaster that follows? People like Jacob Cole, MP? Or people like her?*

Ricky found himself looking at the old bag lady. Then he stared around the café at the other customers. And he realized that the voice in his head was right. It wasn't Felix he had just deserted – it was ordinary people who knew nothing of what was going on. Ordinary people like his mum and dad and Madeleine, if they had lived. He couldn't help them; but he *could* try and stop anyone else losing their family too . . . try and do the right thing.

– *You want to pretend it's not your problem. But it is now. It's just a question of whether you do anything about it.*

– *I'm not going to force Izzy Cole to go back to her dad. I saw what he did to her.*

– *Maybe she doesn't have to. Maybe there's another way. And in any case, don't you think Izzy should be allowed to make that choice for herself?*

The voice fell silent.

Ricky stirred his hot chocolate. Then, suddenly, he stood up and left, taking his newspaper with him. It might have been his imagination, but he could have sworn that the boy in the baseball cap had caught his eye as he left.

Jacob Cole sat behind his desk in the first-floor study of the White House. Opposite him were two police officers. They were in full uniform and looked rather uncomfortable.

'And you're sure, Mr Cole, that you can think of no reason why Izzy would want to run away?' one of the police officers asked.

Cole's lips grew thin and his eyes narrowed. 'As I have told you and your colleagues more than once,' he said in little more than a whisper, 'my daughter is a rather foolish, extremely hot-headed young lady. It would be just like her to do something silly like this. Now, if I were in *your* position, I would be searching *all night* for my daughter, under every last stone, not sitting here at almost *midnight* asking me *damn fool questions.*' He said these last words with an emphasis that made the two police officers look anxiously at each other. 'I should tell you that I am personally acquainted with the commissioner, and I'm quite prepared to speak to him about the high level of incompetence being demonstrated by this investigation.' Cole stood up and gripped the edge of his desk. '*Find . . . my . . . daughter . . .*' he said. 'Now, it's very late. Please leave.'

The police officers silently stood up and left the room. Cole sat back down again. His blood was boiling with anger. Anger at those idiotic police officers, and anger at his idiotic daughter. Did she have any idea of the problems her stupidity was causing him? Now, of all times, he did not need the glare of publicity shining on him. As it was Christmas, he'd managed to keep Izzy's disappearance out of the newspapers, but for how long?

He took a key from the pocket of his suit jacket and used it to open the top right-hand drawer of his desk. It contained a manila folder. Cole didn't remove it. He didn't even touch it. He just wanted to make sure it was still there. He closed the drawer again and locked it securely.

He stared at the mobile phone on the table, willing it to ring. The sooner he made his deal with the Russians, the better. Once they had the information, they could do what they wanted with it. Cole would have his money, and that was all that mattered.

His wife appeared in the doorway. He noticed that she had been crying again. There were dark streaks under her eyes. She stared at him with loathing, but didn't say anything before disappearing again.

Stupid woman, he thought. Perhaps, when the deal was done, he would leave her, claim that the stress of their daughter running away had forced them apart. Then he would be free to enjoy his money by himself.

Five minutes after leaving the café, Ricky found himself once more outside the entrance to Keeper's House. The snow had stopped and his footprints were the only fresh ones in the street. His breath steamed in the cold, but he felt his blood pumping hard. Returning to Keeper's House was a risk. The Thrownaways could be volatile. More to the point, Hunter didn't fully trust him. He wouldn't want to give him access to Izzy.

But Ricky had to try.

He opened up his newspaper and laid it in the snow. Carefully, he folded it in half several times, just like Felix had taught him, until he had a sturdy truncheon. He gave it a couple of whacks against his open palm. Good and solid. No doubt Hunter and his Thrownaways would have more dangerous weapons than this in their basement, but Ricky felt a little bit better now he had something with which to defend himself.

The main door to Keeper's House was unlocked. It squeaked as he opened it slowly. He crept silently down the stairs into the basement. When he reached the door to the main basement room, he stopped and listened.

Silence.

— Is everyone asleep? Maybe you could wake Izzy without the others knowing . . . ?

Very slowly, he pushed the door open with the tip of his newspaper truncheon.

It was completely dark in the basement and Ricky heard nothing but the gentle rise and fall of heavy breathing. He stayed perfectly still for a minute, allowing his eyes to get used to the blackness. Gradually, he made out dark shapes dotted around the room: furniture, and sleeping bodies.

He found himself automatically dividing the dark room into cubes. He scanned each one carefully, looking for movement.

There was none.

— That doesn't mean they're all asleep. Be very careful. If Hunter finds you in here, he might get violent . . .

He crept inside, his own shallow breath drowning

out the heavy breathing of the others in his ears. He moved very slowly, to keep the sound of his footsteps to a minimum.

Three metres in.

Five metres.

Someone stirred on the far left-hand side of the room. Ricky froze.

Silence again.

He fixed his eyes on the dark, murky outline of the door at the far side of the basement room. It was, he thought, slightly ajar. He started walking again. Creeping, silently, towards it.

– *No!*

From behind, a hand had clamped over his mouth. Ricky's instinct was to shout out in alarm, but he managed to stay quiet, though his muscles tensed up – it was as if they knew they might be needed in a fight. He raised his truncheon, ready to strike if he had to . . .

The hand fell away. Cat-like, his truncheon still aloft, Ricky turned round to find another face centimetres from his.

Tommy.

Tommy's face was hard and suspicious. But he hadn't raised the alarm, and Ricky took that as good news. Very slowly, he lowered his truncheon and raised one finger to his lips.

Very, *very* quietly, Tommy whispered: '*Don't wake Hunter!*' Then he retreated into the darkness. Ricky inhaled deeply to steady his nerves, then kept walking towards the far door. He slipped silently into the next room, then paused for a moment with his back to the door. Having memorized the layout without even thinking about it, he knew from his previous visit that the floor here was littered with mattresses. His sharp eyes picked them out in the darkness and he started to weave his way in and out of them.

Halfway across the room he stopped again. Something told him he was being watched. He looked up and saw a figure standing up with her back against the wall. It was as if Izzy knew he was coming for her. Or maybe she just couldn't sleep and he'd disturbed her when he entered the room? Either way, she hadn't raised the alarm, so Ricky kept walking towards her.

'We need to talk,' he whispered when he was just a couple of metres from where she was standing.

'I'm not going back home,' she breathed.

'I know. Don't worry, I'm not asking you to. But can we just talk? Outside, away from here?'

A pause.

Izzy slowly raised her right hand and Ricky took it. Her hand was icy, and it trembled.

'We need to be quiet. Mustn't wake Hunter,' he murmured.

He carefully led her back to the main basement room, where he tried to pick out Tommy in the darkness, but couldn't. Still holding Izzy's hand, he headed straight for the door.

But he was only halfway there when the room suddenly filled with light.

Dazzled, Ricky covered his eyes with his right arm, which was still holding the newspaper truncheon. He uncovered them a fraction of a second later, because he had heard Izzy scream.

Hunter was there, five metres away, bearing down on them like a madman. His eyes were wild and angry, his leathery face curled into a vicious snarl. In his right hand he held a wicked-looking knife. Ricky's mind flashed back to the last time someone had drawn a knife on him: the witch-like woman in Bloomsbury Square. Back then, he'd had Felix to rescue him. But now he was on his own.

'Run!' he barked at Izzy. She staggered towards the door. Ricky was aware of the other Thrownaways drowsily waking up. He had to deal with Hunter before any of them decided to come to the man's aid.

Three metres between them. Hunter was raising his arm, ready to strike.

How had Felix dealt with the witch? Ricky

pictured that scene. He'd gone for the wrist of her knife hand with his stick.

Ricky had no stick. But he did have the truncheon.

He moved almost on instinct. Hunter was almost upon him now, just about to strike with the knife. With a sudden movement, Ricky whacked the truncheon against Hunter's knife hand with all the force he could muster. It connected sharply. Hunter roared out in pain, and the knife went clattering to the floor.

– *GET OUT OF HERE! NOW!*

Ricky spun round. Izzy was already at the door, but she was staring towards them, her eyes wide and horrified.

'Move!' Ricky shouted, and he sprinted in her direction as Hunter, still roaring with pain, scrambled to pick up the knife.

'*Get 'em!*' Hunter yelled. Suddenly Ricky was aware that at least ten of the Thrownaways were on their feet. Tommy was one of them, but he was holding back, clearly reluctant to try to catch Ricky. But Ricky knew that if Hunter forced him, he wouldn't have a choice. None of them would.

Izzy was halfway up the stairs now and Ricky was already by the door. But Hunter and the Thrownaways were bearing down on him, and some of them had knives – there was no way he could deal with them all using just a rolled-up newspaper.

Again, instinct took over. He dropped the truncheon and plunged one hand into the pocket of his jeans. When he removed it, he was clutching a handful of coins.

'You can't pay your way out of this one, sunshine,' Hunter snarled.

Ricky ignored the threat. What had Felix said? *If I throw a handful of coins hard enough at your face, you're going to know about it . . .*

Ricky didn't hesitate. He hurled the coins towards Hunter and his boys, as hard as he could. As he turned his back on them, he heard several of them shouting in pain. But he was already clattering up the steps after Izzy, taking two steps at a time. He looked over his shoulder. One of the Thrownaways – a small kid with ginger hair – was already at the bottom of the stairs. 'Move!' Ricky hissed at Izzy. '*Move!*'

Five seconds later, they burst out of Keeper's House. Izzy was already out of breath, but they couldn't stop now. He grabbed her by the hand and yanked her towards the end of the street.

'They're following!' she cried as they turned right onto Berwick Street. '*They're following us!*'

'Keep running,' Ricky hissed. And then he added: '*In a straight line!*'

They sprinted down the slidy, snowy road. Every ten paces or so, Ricky would lose his grip and slip. But somehow he and Izzy managed to keep each other up. The further they ran towards Piccadilly, the more people they encountered. And after three or four minutes, Ricky stopped and looked back, his lungs burning.

'We've lost them,' he panted.

Izzy was gasping for air. She was shivering too. Hardly surprising. Even though they'd been running, it was freezing outside.

'Let's get a hot drink,' he said.

Izzy nodded gratefully, then said: 'You're really *not* going to tell my dad where I am, right?'

Ricky gave her a serious kind of look. 'Let's talk,' he said. He checked again for any sign of pursuing Thrownaways, but there were none. And so without another word, he took her hand and led her into a nearby McDonald's.

15

THE BLIND SPOT

McDonald's wasn't busy. It was gone midnight on Boxing Day, after all. A few drunk youths were making a noise in the far corner and everyone else in the restaurant – there were fifteen or twenty others – kept their distance and did their best not to look in that direction. Ricky told Izzy to take a seat near the door, and kept half an eye on her as he went to buy hot tea, burgers and fries with the last of his remaining loose change. He didn't want her to run off.

But she didn't. When he placed the food in front of her, she devoured it hungrily. While she ate, Ricky looked out of the window. London was still busy, despite the late hour and the snow. A red bus trundled past, a line of traffic close behind. Everyone was driving carefully in the bad weather.

Ricky watched a well-wrapped-up cyclist wobble past, then noticed a second cyclist on the other side of the road – his bike was propped up against a street lamp and he had crouched down to fix something on the drive chain.

Ricky's senses were immediately ultra-alert. What had Felix told him? *Nobody looks twice at a cyclist fiddling with his chain. It means you can stay in the same place, watching and waiting, for ages.*

– *It's probably just a regular cyclist*, said the voice in his head. *You're being paranoid.* But Ricky took careful note of the cyclist's clothes – black puffa jacket, red scarf. If he saw that figure again, he'd know to be suspicious . . .

He turned back to Izzy and couldn't help staring at her. She was so like Madeleine. He waited until she had drunk half of her steaming hot tea before even asking her a question.

'Do you think your dad is up to anything dodgy?'

He watched her face carefully as he said this, looking for any flicker of surprise or annoyance. There was none. But she didn't answer. She just took another sip of her tea and stared at him over the brim of the cup.

'*I* think he is,' said Ricky.

Izzy put the cup down. 'How would you know that?'

'Let's just say I've got a source.'

'A good source?'

Ricky thought of Felix, limping furiously around the apartment, and all that he had said.

'Yeah,' he replied. 'A very good source.'

Izzy bowed her head. 'He's a monster,' she whispered. 'He only thinks about himself.'

'Can you remember anything he has ever said about' – Ricky lowered his voice slightly – 'nuclear location codes, or any dealings he's had with Russians?'

Izzy's eyes widened and she nodded her head. 'I heard him shouting down the phone. It was just a few hours before I ran away. He was talking to someone called Dmitri, saying that this Dmitri guy wouldn't get anything until Dad got his money first.'

'How did he sound when he was talking?' Ricky asked.

'Really angry. He had a massive argument with Mum afterwards.' She looked down again and touched the side of her still-bruised face. 'That was when he did *this*.'

Ricky had to hold down a feeling of contempt for this man who would hit his daughter like that. But he put that from his mind as he tried to decide how he was going to explain everything to Izzy.

– You could try the truth.

– She'd never believe it.

– Then tell her as much as you think she will *believe.*

Ricky frowned. 'There are these people,' he said. 'They think your dad's doing something wrong. They wanted me to find you and persuade you to go back home so you can spy on him and get hard evidence of what he's up to.'

Izzy was already sliding off her chair, her eyes a bit wild, getting ready to run. Ricky grabbed her wrist. 'I told them I wouldn't do it. Nobody's sending you back home, not if you don't want to go. That's a promise.'

The girl seemed to relax a little. She sat down again.

'But listen,' Ricky continued. 'This thing they're accusing your dad of, it's really bad. It could hurt a lot of people. I thought . . . I thought, maybe . . .' Now that he had to say it, Ricky's plan sounded stupid. But it was the only plan he had, so he blurted it out. 'I thought you could tell *me* a good way to break into your parents' house. Maybe I can, you know, *find* something.'

Izzy looked around nervously, then stared at him. 'If my dad gets his hands on you . . .' she whispered.

'I know,' Ricky said quietly. 'Look, if you don't want to do it . . .'

'Might he go to prison?' Izzy asked, her voice suddenly fierce.

Ricky thought about that for a moment. 'Yeah,' he said. 'I think so. Then you could move back in with your mum.'

But Izzy shook her head. 'No way. She's just as bad. She *let* him do this to me.' A determined look crossed her face. 'There are security cameras covering the outside of the house,' she told him. 'Front, back, everywhere. Dad thinks he's got the whole house covered, but there's a blind spot. It's possible to get from the bottom of the garden up to the back door of the house without being seen, if you know the route. And, *and*' – she was almost getting excited now – 'I dropped a back-door key in the snow when I left. It's probably still there . . .'

'Can you tell me what the route is?'

Izzy nodded. 'Of course. From the gate at the bottom of the garden you go about ten paces forward till you get to this kind of bird-bath thing, then—' She suddenly fell silent. 'It's too hard to describe,' she said. 'I can walk it with my eyes closed, but that's only because I've been doing it since I was a little kid. Like a kind of game.'

Disappointed, Ricky nodded. He looked out of the window onto Shaftesbury Avenue. The buses were still passing and the cyclist in the black puffa jacket was still adjusting his bike. A fresh layer of snow was falling.

Snow.

It gave him an idea.

He turned back to Izzy.

'I need to ask you a favour,' he said.

Jacob Cole, MP, sat alone in his office. It was very late and he was very tired. But they *still* hadn't called. He stared at the mobile phone on his desk in front of him, willing it to ring. It didn't.

He looked at his watch. One o'clock in the morning. How much longer would he have to wait for those accursed Russians to make contact?

He sighed heavily, then stood up and walked to the window. His office looked out over the garden, dark and thick with snow. He wondered where his daughter was, in weather like this. It would be her own fault if the stupid girl was freezing. After everything he'd done for her.

He sat down at the desk again, and continued to stare at his phone. What if it ran out of charge? He plugged it into the charger – there was no way he would miss the call when it came . . .

Izzy looked horrified at Ricky's suggestion. He knew he'd have to talk fast to persuade her.

'You won't have to enter the house, I promise. And if anything goes wrong, I'll help you escape.'

Izzy closed her eyes. 'OK,' she said quickly, as if scared that she might change her mind. 'OK. When do we do it?'

'How does now suit you?'

'*Now?*'

'It's important, Izzy. I've got the feeling we don't have much time to lose.'

Forty-five minutes later, they were standing in a narrow, deserted alleyway in the centre of Mayfair. Izzy was trembling, but Ricky suspected that was nothing to do with the cold. Five metres to their right there was a heavy gate, but Izzy was examining the brick wall beside it. 'About here,' she murmured. She bent down and rummaged in the snow. A moment later she straightened up. She was holding a key, which she handed to Ricky. 'That will get you into the kitchen,' she said. 'There's an alarm, but they don't turn it on while they're in the house – the outside security cameras are the main thing.' She looked up to the top of the wall. 'You can't see it, but there's barbed wire. We'll both have to be careful.'

Ricky nodded. 'I'll give you a leg-up,' he said.

With Ricky holding her foot, Izzy easily climbed the wall, then swung her legs over the top to avoid the wire. It was harder for Ricky and he found himself wishing that his lessons from Felix had included learning how to scale a wall. But they hadn't, so he had to make do. He turned his Nike cap so it was pointing backwards again, out of the way, and jumped as high as he could, grabbing the top of the snow-covered wall with his fingertips, then pulling himself up with all his strength. His muscles burned by the time his head was level with the top of the wall. He kept straining, and a few seconds later he too was swinging his legs over the top, trying to avoid the wire but snagging his jeans and adding another rip to them at one point. He landed with a thump next to Izzy.

She was crouching in the snow, looking towards the house, which was large and imposing. The lights of all the rooms were switched off, except one in the centre of the house on the first floor. Its window was long and rectangular, floor to ceiling, and vertical blinds were pulled so they could see a figure standing there, looking out over the garden. The light from the room shone down onto the pure, untouched blanket of snow below, and the figure cast an elongated shadow.

Ricky groaned inwardly. He had been relying on the whole house being asleep.

'Is that your dad?' he breathed.

Izzy nodded silently. She was still shaking. He

grabbed her hand. 'He's in the light, we're in the dark. He can't see us, OK? And look up, there's no moon visible, but lots of cloud. We will be as good as invisible.' He wasn't sure he totally believed this, but he did need to convince Izzy.

'OK.' Izzy's voice was slightly hoarse. 'Shouldn't we wait until he's asleep?'

Ricky considered that. It could mean waiting all night, and they'd freeze crouching here for that long. Plus, Izzy could easily change her mind about all this in the morning.

'No. We need to go through with it now. Who else is likely to be in the house?'

'Just my mum,' Izzy said. 'She'll be asleep, I'm sure of it.' She glanced downwards. 'She takes these sleeping tablets—'

'And there's no, what do you call it, staff?' he interrupted her.

Izzy shook her head. 'Not at night.'

'OK. Where's your mum and dad's bedroom?'

'They sleep in separate rooms. Hers is on the second floor at the top of the stairs. You see the dormer window? That's it. She has her own dressing room on the other side of the house.'

'And what's that room where your dad is?'

'His office. He sleeps in the bedroom next door.' She suddenly gave him a sharp look. 'Have you done this sort of thing before? You sound like you know what you're doing.' She swallowed. 'My dad . . . he's doing something really awful, isn't he?'

He blinked at her, but didn't answer. In his head, though, he heard Felix's voice. *You've already shown me time and again that you have a very high degree of aptitude for the work involved. Your attitude is a different matter, of course, but we can work on that . . .*

'You're sure this part of the garden isn't covered by the security cameras?' he asked instead.

'Positive.'

'And you can get to the kitchen door without being seen?'

She nodded.

They waited. Ricky kept his eyes fixed on the figure in the window. It stood motionless for a couple of minutes, then turned and walked further into the room. The light stayed on, but he could sense Izzy relaxing slightly.

'Are you ready?'

Another nod.

'Then go. Make sure you leave very clear foot-prints in the snow.'

Izzy swallowed hard. She stood up. 'You'll be here?'

'All the time.'

She headed left along the wall, ten paces, before turning right into the main body of the garden. Ricky kept one eye on her as she weaved round a little vegetable patch. He kept the other eye on the window, and he thought he could make out movement in the room – the flicker of a shadow pacing up and down – but the window itself remained clear.

Now Izzy was creeping past an old swing towards a flower bed. She was alongside the house and gingerly picking her way up to the kitchen door, where she stopped. Ricky watched as she looked back in his direction, peering but clearly unable to see him. She did an about turn, then followed her tracks back along her exact route, glancing over her shoulder every few minutes to see if her father had reappeared.

When she was back by the swing, he did.

Izzy froze. So did Ricky.

Jacob Cole stared out of the window for what seemed like an age. Ricky zoomed in on him with his sharp eyes. The man looked like he was scanning the garden.

Had he seen Izzy? Did he think there was an intruder? Would he see the footprints in the snow? Thank goodness the clouds were hiding the moon . . .

Cole disappeared back into the room and Izzy started moving again, quicker this time. She was obviously freaked. When she reached Ricky her breath came in short, terrified gasps.

'Do you think he saw me?'

Ricky looked back towards the window. He could see the moving shadow inside again. 'No,' he whispered. 'I don't think he did.' He turned back to Izzy. 'I can take it from here,' he said. 'If you want to leave.'

She looked up to the top of the wall, then back to her father's window. Ricky expected her to go, but she shook her head. 'I'll stay here. Just in case . . .'

'OK. But if it looks like everything's going wrong, don't wait for your dad to catch you. Get out of here.'

'Ricky?'

'What is it?'

'What are you looking for, exactly? I mean, I know you want evidence that my dad's doing something bad, but what would that look like?'

It was a question that had been bothering Ricky, and he answered as honestly as he could. 'I don't know. I'm just hoping I recognize it when I see it.' He found himself half wondering why he was doing this alone, without Felix's help. A quick glance at Izzy, and her remarkable similarity to his dead sister, reminded him. This was for her, not Felix and his crew.

Without waiting for a reply, he readjusted his cap so that his face would be hidden by the peak, then turned and followed the tracks Izzy had left in the snow. He moved very carefully, making sure that his footsteps matched Izzy's prints exactly. Past the vegetable patch . . . past the swing . . . past the flower bed . . .

– *Stop! Don't move! He's there!*

He was indeed, staring out of the window. Closer now, Ricky could make out his features better. The thin, pinched, unfriendly face. The searching eyes. He stayed absolutely still for a full minute, until Jacob Cole disappeared from his window once again.

He continued to follow Izzy's footsteps, carefully placing his own feet in the impressions they had left in the snow. Moments later, he was outside the kitchen door.

He looked back. To his relief he saw that Izzy was entirely hidden at the bottom of the garden. But he could once more see Jacob Cole's shadow on the snow, framed in the rectangular patch of light from the window. He had the sense that Cole was nervous – all this pacing and staring out of the window. But why?

He retrieved the key Izzy had picked out of the snow from his pocket and slid it into the keyhole. It opened easily. Ricky stepped into the kitchen and quietly closed the door behind him.

He was in.

16

SNEAK THIEF

— This is crazy. What are you even doing here?

— Snooping.

— If they catch you, it'll mean the police. Felix won't help you. You've walked out on him and he doesn't even know what you're doing.

— Then I'd better make sure they don't catch me.

Ricky allowed his eyes to adjust to the darkness of the kitchen. He could smell the remnants of whatever meal had been cooked in here last, and he suddenly realized how hungry he was. He'd let Izzy eat most of the food in McDonald's — she had needed it more than him.

— Keep your mind on the job. You're here to find incriminating evidence on Jacob Cole, not steal from the pantry.

He made to lock the kitchen door again, but once

more he heard Felix's voice crack in his mind. *You always want an escape route.* So he left the door unlocked, and tiptoed across the kitchen. He was aware of snow falling from his shoes and trousers, but it instantly melted into puddles on the heated floor.

There was a loud creaking sound. He stopped statue still, his heart pumping fast.

– *It's an old house. You're going to get noises like that at night.*

Ricky breathed again and continued to the door on the opposite side of the kitchen. He opened it slightly, and looked out onto an oak-panelled hallway with a large Christmas tree. The lights were still twinkling, and Ricky felt a pang as he remembered Christmases in his past life, with his mum and dad. Those days had long since passed. There were still gifts under the tree – Izzy's, Ricky assumed. He wondered how long they would stay there.

There was a sweeping staircase bending out of sight from the main hallway, but also a door to another dark room. Ricky crept past the Christmas tree and into this room.

Creak!

He froze again.

– *Just the h—*

– *Yeah, I know, it's just the house.*

He was in a large living room. Sofas, a fireplace. The curtains were closed, but this room obviously looked out onto the street because it was suddenly half lit up by the headlamps of a passing car. The lights made Ricky's shadow seem massive against the wall, but they died away very quickly.

To the right of the fireplace was a writing desk. Ricky tiptoed towards it and, using the cube method Felix had taught him, swiftly examined all the drawers. He found nothing except blank stationery, a bottle of ink and some paperclips. He scanned the room again for anywhere that might conceal in-criminating documents, but there was none, so he quietly left.

At the foot of the staircase he looked up and listened hard. Silence. Should he head upstairs? Jacob Cole was still awake and about. The closer Ricky went to that room with the light on, the higher his chance of being caught . . . He took another deep breath and crept upstairs.

On the landing, he could see light seeping from around the door to Jacob Cole's study. It was the third door on the right – one of many that led off this long, broad landing. Along the landing itself he saw an elegant, old-fashioned sofa with curved wooden legs and, opposite it, a small marble statue on a pedestal. Above him, the stairs wound up to the next floor where he knew Izzy's mum would be sleeping. He considered following them up, and searching the house from the top down. He knew, in his gut, that if he was going to find anything to incriminate Jacob Cole, he would find it in that office. But then he remembered what Felix had once told him when he'd failed to find that tiny key in his apartment. *Forgive me, but if you'd looked everywhere, you'd have found it.*

– *You need to look everywhere.*

Silently he headed up the stairs.

The second-floor landing was smaller than the first and Ricky realized he was in the converted loft of the house. There was a faint smell of perfume in the air, and of the two doors leading from the landing, one was slightly ajar. He walked up to it and peered through the darkness into the room. He saw the outline of a bed, and heard heavy breathing – that had to be Izzy's mum's room. What were the chances of finding incriminating evidence in there? Small, he decided, and in any case: to wander around someone's bedroom while they were asleep was incredibly risky.

He backed off and headed over to the second door. It creaked as he opened it. Ricky slipped inside and stood very still as he waited to see if the noise had woken anybody up.

Silence.

He peered through the gloom. There was a dressing table with a mirror at one end of the room. Thick, warm carpet. Rails of clothes on either side. And it was from in here that the smell of perfume came.

– Izzy's mum's dressing room?

– Looks like it.

– You should head back downstairs. This is all clothes and jewellery.

Jewellery. Ricky found his eyes fixed on the dressing table at the far end of the room. He approached it quietly. There were several jewellery boxes on its surface.

– Old habits die hard, eh?

Ricky ignored the voice in his head. He selected the largest of the jewellery boxes and undid the clasp on the top. It concertina'd open to present three layers, each full of necklaces. He felt his eyes bulging in the darkness. There had to be hundreds of thousands of pounds worth of jewellery in this box alone.

He would only take one item, he decided. The loss of all this jewellery would indicate a break-in, whereas the loss of a single necklace could be explained away in other ways – and maybe not even noticed.

– So Felix was wrong. You are just a sneak thief.

Ricky selected an elegant necklace dripping with diamonds. There was no time to admire it. He simply shoved it into his rucksack and closed the jewellery box. Moments later, he was creeping out of the dressing room and back onto the second-floor landing. He could still hear the heavy breathing of Izzy's mum. Clearly he hadn't disturbed her. But he decided he was wasting his time up here. He needed to get back down to the first floor and into Jacob Cole's office if he was going to find anything of use.

The trouble was, Cole was in there too. From his vantage point on the stairs, he could still see the light escaping from the door frame of the office.

Ricky decided that he would just have to wait. Let Cole go to bed, then silently gain access to the study and search it at his leisure.

He looked up and down the landing for some-where to hide. Behind that elegant sofa perhaps? Or maybe he should sneak into one of the other rooms. Maybe he should—

He froze.

Cole had suddenly turned off the light in the study and Ricky could hear footsteps heading towards the door. Light-footed, he ran past the office and crouched down behind the far end of the sofa. He peered over the edge of the armrest just in time to see the office door open. The figure of Jacob Cole stepped out into the corridor.

Ricky held his breath as he watched the silhouette of Izzy's dad. He hadn't yet closed the door behind him, but was standing in the corridor, perfectly still.

He looked left, towards the stairs.

Had he heard something? Did he know there was an intruder?

Then he looked right, towards Ricky.

– If you move, even just a few centimetres, he'll see you.

For once, Ricky didn't answer the voice in his head back. He concentrated on remaining absolutely still.

Jacob Cole continued staring in his direction for what seemed like minutes. In reality, Ricky knew, it was probably only a few seconds before he turned again and closed the office door. There was the solid clunk of a latch closing. Then Jacob Cole walked a few metres along the corridor to his own bedroom. He entered and shut himself inside. A faint glow of light seeped from the edge of the bedroom door-frame.

Ricky didn't move for a full five minutes. His palms were sweaty with nerves, and half of him wanted to run as quickly as possible back to the kitchen door and get out of there. But he knew, deep down, that he was at least going to try to search the office, and that meant waiting a little longer. So he waited until the light spill from Cole's bedroom disappeared before he stood up and – very slowly – crept to the office door.

Silently, carefully, he tried the handle.

Locked.

Ricky cursed inwardly.

– *What kind of lock is it?*

He touched the key hole underneath the handle. It was a Yale lock. That meant he could use his snap gun.

Ricky quietly took his rucksack from his shoulder, removed the snap gun, then shouldered the bag again. He glanced towards Cole's bedroom and strained his ears to listen for any sound of movement.

None.

Moving very slowly so he didn't make any unnecessary noise, he slid the blade of the snap gun into the lock. The clicking sound as he pumped the trigger sounded unnaturally loud and it made his palms sweat even more.

– *Open it quickly, otherwise you'll disturb him.*

– *I'm going as quick as I can . . .*

He had it open in thirty seconds. Not for the first time that evening, Ricky found himself thankful for the training Felix had given him. With a final glance towards the bedroom, he slipped inside the office and, after double-checking that he could easily open the door from inside, he closed it behind him.

Thanks to the enormous floor-to-ceiling windows and the bright white snow outside, Ricky could see quite well, even though the light was off. He gave himself a few seconds to take in the layout of the room. There was a large desk at one end with a leather chair on the far side, and two much less comfortable-looking chairs facing it. The walls were lined with wooden bookcases while an enormous antique globe stood on a pedestal in one corner. He crept over to the window – vertical blinds were pulled wide open – and looked out onto the garden. There was no sign of Izzy crouching by the wall, and he couldn't make out the tracks in the snow, which was a relief.

He turned his attention to the desk. It was very neat. Ricky stepped round the two chairs facing it and examined a photograph in a silver frame which sat on one side of the desk. He half expected to see a picture of Izzy, but no: it showed Cole himself standing alongside the Prime Minister, and smiling. It was the kind of smile that made you feel a bit creepy. Next to the picture there was a notepad and a biro. Ricky flicked through the pad, but Cole hadn't written anything on it.

In the middle of the desk, Cole had left his mobile phone plugged into a charger. With slightly trembling fingers, Ricky made to pick it up. But before his fingers made contact, he stopped. He examined the exact angle at which the phone was lying on the desk. It would be sloppy of him to pick it up and return it in a different position.

He picked it up. It was slightly warm, which suggested to Ricky that Cole had been using it very recently, either to talk to someone or to access the internet.

– There could be helpful information on that phone. Recently dialled numbers, websites he's accessed.

He swiped the home screen. The phone asked him for a passcode, and he had no way of knowing what it might be. Ricky allowed himself a wry smile. He hadn't really expected it to be as easy as that . . .

He returned the phone to its place on the desk, then sat down in the comfortable leather chair and turned his attention to the drawers.

There were four on either side of the desk. The top drawer on the right-hand side was locked. The others were all open, so Ricky quietly opened them one by one and searched their contents, but like the desk downstairs these drawers contained nothing of interest – items of stationery, old passport photos, and two of the drawers were entirely empty.

Ricky turned his attention to the locked drawer. His forefinger traced the outline of the little Chubb keyhole. The snap gun would be no good for that. The only way he was going to find out what was in it was by finding a key.

He smiled another wry smile as he remembered again his very first lesson with Felix.

Could the key to this locked drawer be hidden somewhere in the room? Almost instinctively, he looked around the room and started dividing the space into cubes. How long, he wondered, would it take him to search the entire place? An hour? Maybe a little more?

Ricky started. A door slammed in the corridor outside and he heard footsteps. A thin strip of light appeared at the bottom of the door.

– Cole is out of bed!

For a fraction of a second, Ricky felt paralysed. Only when he saw the shadow of footsteps passing – and clearing – the door did he regain control of his muscles.

– He's probably just going to the loo. He won't come back in here.

– You should hide anyway. Just in case.

Ricky looked desperately around the room,

searching for hiding places. There were none – no curtains to stand behind, no bulky items of furniture except the desk at which he sat . . .

He felt a moment of panic. But that panic only doubled when, a second later, the mobile phone on the desk started to ring.

It was loud. Very loud. As well as the ring tone, the phone buzzed noisily against the hard wooden surface of the table. Its screen lit up, illuminating the whole room. It said: 'Caller Unknown'. Each time it rang, it slid about half a centimetre along the desk.

– *You need to hide! HIDE!*

All of a sudden, the sound of the mobile was not the only thing causing panic in Ricky's mind. As soon as it had started ringing there were heavy foot-steps in the corridor. Running. A clattering on the other side of the door as someone placed a key into the lock.

Ricky had no option. As the phone continued to ring and someone – Cole, presumably – tried to gain access to the room, he sank to the floor and wormed his way underneath the desk. He huddled himself up into a ball so he took up as little space as possible. If anyone looked under the desk, they'd see him immediately. But if their attention was else-where, maybe he had a chance . . .

The door opened. Ricky's eyes burned suddenly

as the lights were switched on. The phone continued to ring. Through his suddenly dazzled vision, Ricky saw legs walking – running – towards the desk from the door. Their owner was wearing a dressing gown and slippers, but Ricky could make out his knobbly ankles and thin shins.

A metre out from the desk, the owner of those legs almost threw himself towards the phone. There was a great clatter as he knocked the two chairs onto their side. Ricky held his breath as the ringing stopped and a male voice said, 'Hello? *Hello?* Yes, this is Cole. You're late, you were supposed to phone two hours ago.'

Ricky didn't dare move. Cole was standing right by the table, no more than thirty centimetres from where he was crouched underneath. Ricky silently begged him not to move, or start pacing. The further he walked from the desk and into the main part of the room, the more likely he was to see Ricky hiding. And if he bent down to pick up the fallen chairs, they'd come face to face . . .

Sweat poured from Ricky's crunched-up body. He wished he hadn't stolen the necklace, but he put that from his mind as he listened to the conversation going on above him.

'Tomorrow, you say? Yes, I can do tomorrow.'

– *Do* what *tomorrow?*

'You want to come *here*? Are you out of your mind, Dmitri? That would be entirely inappropriate. If anybody *saw* you . . .'

Dmitri. That had been the name Izzy had mentioned.

'Absolutely not,' Cole continued. 'We shall meet at a location of *my* choosing, not of yours.' There was another pause as he thought for a moment. 'There is a café off the Kilburn High Road. It's called the Happy Valley Café. I will be there at precisely nine a.m. in the morning. We will make the exchange then. Make sure you have the money, Dmitri, because I will not suffer any foolishness.'

Ricky could faintly hear the voice at the other end of the line, but it was suddenly cut short as Cole hung up. Then there was a clattering sound as he dropped the phone back onto the table.

Ricky's lungs ached from holding his breath. Very slowly, he breathed out. Then in again. To his own ears, his breath sounded like a gale. He kept his eyes fixed on Jacob Cole's lower leg. The man didn't move. Ricky pictured him staring at the phone and considering the conversation that he'd just had. Ricky was wondering about that too. Who was this Dmitri? Why didn't Cole want him near his house? What would they be exchanging at the Happy Valley Café? What was the money for?

Yet again, Felix's voice echoed in his head. *There are terrorists, or members of rogue states, who would pay a great deal of money for nuclear submarine location codes. And they would only pay such sums if they were prepared to use the information . . .*

– Leave! Please leave!

Jacob Cole stood by his desk for a full minute. Without any warning, he walked round to the other side and sat down on the leather chair.

Ricky shrank away from Cole's legs, which were now underneath the table, just centimetres from him. He heard the sound of a key in the lock. The sliding of a drawer. The fluttering of papers.

Thirty seconds passed. The drawer slid shut again. The lock clicked.

– Did he put the papers back in the drawer?

– What does it matter? We didn't hear him searching for his key. That means he must have had it on him. We're never going to break into that drawer.

As this conversation took place in Ricky's head, Cole stood up, walked round to the other side of the desk and headed towards the door.

– He's leaving.

Ricky allowed himself another lungful of air as relief flooded over him.

It didn't last.

Halfway to the door, Cole suddenly stopped.

He turned.

Ricky could see Cole from the waist down now. But could Cole see *him*?

Ten seconds passed. They felt like ten hours.

'It's nothing,' Cole muttered under his breath. He turned again and walked to the door. As he opened it, he switched off the light. Then he left the room and allowed the door to clunk heavily behind him.

17

NI

Ricky's blood ran hot and cold. He realized how close he'd just come to being caught. But he also realized, as he remained crouched in the darkness beneath Jacob Cole's desk, that he had a lead.

– *What do we do? Call Felix and tell him?*

– *No way. I'm done with Felix. He wanted to send Izzy back to her father, remember? If we're going to get some dirt on Jacob Cole, we have to do it by ourselves. Otherwise Felix will just want to send her back home again.*

First things first. He had to get out of here. He waited, huddled in the darkness, for another ten minutes. Only when everything in the house was silent again did he venture out from under the desk. The phone was still lying there. Perhaps he should steal it? No. If he did, Cole would realize there had been an intruder. Ricky wasn't quite sure what his next move was going to be, but he knew this: if Cole suspected he had been overheard, it would make everything more difficult. He tried the top drawer for a second time, just on the off-chance. No luck. It was locked again.

So he tiptoed towards the door and listened carefully for a moment before opening it. The landing was dark and empty. He edged towards the staircase, resisting the urge to run and get out of the house as quickly as possible. He padded down the stairs, wincing every time the floorboards creaked. In the hallway, he briefly thought about taking one of the smaller presents from under the tree to give to Izzy. She wasn't having much of a Christmas, after all. But no. He'd already taken too much of a risk in stealing the jewellery from Izzy's mum. In fact, he was beginning to wish he hadn't done that. It was too late to return it, though. His top priority had to be getting out of here.

The kitchen seemed colder than when he'd entered the house. Or perhaps that was just him. He headed to the back door and stepped outside, then closed and locked the door behind him before retracing his footsteps back across the garden. He took very good care not to deviate from Izzy's footsteps, and two minutes later he had re-joined her.

She was freezing cold. Shivering. Blue lips. A thin layer of snow over her head and clothes. But she managed to ask him: 'Did you find anything?'

'Maybe. You going to be OK?'

She nodded weakly, but it was clear to Ricky that she needed to get warm, and fast. He helped her clamber back over the wall. Then he climbed over himself. Back in the snow-filled alleyway, Ricky grabbed Izzy's hand. He forced her to run, more to warm her up than anything. They weaved their way onto Park Lane, then up towards Marble Arch. In the shadow of that stone arch, Izzy tugged on his arm to stop him. He looked at her to see that she was crying.

'I can't go back to Hunter's, can I?'

Ricky shook his head grimly. 'I get the impression he doesn't take too kindly to people disobeying him. But it was only a matter of time before he sent you out onto the street with all the others. You don't want to end up like that.'

'Where am I going to go?' she whispered. 'I haven't got any money – Hunter took it all . . .'

Ricky frowned. She was right. Hunter's had been a bad place, but it had been a roof over Izzy's head, and protection from the warmth. For a moment he considered taking her back to the apartment where he'd been living for the past few months. Making his peace with Felix. But no. Felix would have no qualms about sending Izzy back to her dad, and Ricky had promised her that wouldn't happen.

But where could she go? Where could she stay? There were homeless shelters across London, of course, but if she turned up at one of those, they would ask questions, speak to the authorities. And there were other pockets of Thrownaways across the capital, but he couldn't let her fall in with them. Sooner or later, she'd find her way back to Hunter, or someone like him.

'I'm not going back home,' she whispered, as if that was going to be Ricky's next suggestion.

'I know,' Ricky said quietly. 'I understand.' But in the quiet of his mind, he wondered if Izzy would change her mind if her dad was out of the way . . .

The problem, as always, was money. Ricky would gladly give her what he could spare. But that wouldn't be enough to get accommodation for long, even if Izzy could find somewhere a minor could live unreported. But they needed to get warm, and Ricky needed time to think. He took her hand again. 'Come with me,' he said.

At the bottom of the Edgware Road they hailed a night bus. It was busy – they only just managed to find themselves seats at the very back. But it was at least warm. After five minutes, Izzy stopped shivering. She wiped away the condensation on the inside of the window and looked out at the dark London street.

'Public transport is good,' Ricky said. He spoke quietly, so the other passengers couldn't hear – not that any of them were paying any attention. 'You can buy a ticket that lasts you all day, which is much cheaper than staying in some dodgy guest house. It's always warm on the underground or on a bus. Nobody asks you any questions and it's safer than the streets.' He put his hand in his back pocket and pulled out three twenty-pound notes – almost the last of his money now. He pressed two of them into Izzy's hand. 'We'll stay on night buses till the underground opens,' he said. 'Then we'll get some breakfast and you can buy an all-day ticket for the tube. I'll meet you in the Piccadilly Circus ticket office at midday, if I can. There's a newspaper kiosk opposite the exit to Regent Street.'

'What do you mean, if you can?'

Ricky gave her a serious look. 'I've got things to do. I don't know how they'll pan out. If I miss our meeting, then we'll turn up at the same place, same time the following day. You've enough money for food and night bus tickets to get you through the night. Just don't go back to Hunter, OK? Oh, and stick some of this in your shoe – keep it safe from any pickpockets.'

She looked very unsure, but she nodded, and went back to looking out of the window. Ricky closed his eyes and allowed himself a few moments' sleep. In just a few hours, he had an appointment at the Happy Valley Café, and he would need his wits about him.

– *You could speed dial one. Call Felix in. He could take it from here.*

– *No way. What if the meeting's totally innocent? I'd look stupid.*

– *Pride, Ricky?*

– *Maybe.*

But Ricky was honest enough with himself to admit that it was more than that. This was for Izzy, not Felix. But maybe it was for Ricky himself as well. Because if he could save Izzy on his own then maybe – just maybe – he could stop feeling guilty about Madeleine . . .

Jacob Cole had woken at dawn, as usual. Ordinarily, he would put on a crisp, clean shirt, a sober tie and a well-cut suit. In Westminster, these were the kind of clothes that made him blend in. Not today. His nine o'clock meeting would take him to a place where a well-cut suit would attract unwanted stares.

He even felt a bit uncomfortable that the jeans he hardly ever wore had a designer label. He decided that he would leave his shirt untucked – something he usually didn't approve of – to cover it up.

At eight a.m. he stepped out of his dressing room and glanced up the stairs to where his wife was still sleeping. Those tablets of hers would keep her unconscious until at least ten, by which time the deal would be done. Cole felt a little surge of excitement at that thought. Just two hours until he had more money than he could ever hope to spend.

He stepped into his office, but before retrieving his papers from the desk, he stood at the window for a moment, watching the snow fall thickly over his large garden. He remembered Izzy, when she was a toddler, running up and down the garden, squealing as the water from a sprinkler hit her. His lip curled. How had such a pretty little child turned into such an ungrateful wretch?

He frowned. Looking out over the garden, he thought he saw tracks in the snow. They seemed to lead up to the kitchen door, past the vegetable patch and down towards the garden wall. The falling snow had covered them up somewhat, but they were still there. He supposed an urban fox must have found its way into the garden, and he would have to speak to the gardeners about that. There must be some way of trapping and killing the blasted things.

He turned away from the window and walked to the desk. His mobile phone was still there, now showing a full charge. He put it in his pocket and opened up the top drawer of the desk. The valuable papers were still safely hidden inside. He took them out, briefly looked through them for a final time, and then sealed them inside a briefcase which was propped against the far wall of the room. He set the numerical lock on the briefcase – 839 462 – then locked it securely.

Before leaving the room, he glanced out of the window again. Something about the fox made him uncomfortable. The trail from the bottom of the garden to the kitchen door was very roundabout. If it *had* been a fox, surely it would have taken a more direct route.

Cole felt an anxious chill. Something wasn't right.

He strode from the room, tightly gripping the suitcase, and headed down the stairs two at a time. He hurried past the Christmas tree and into the kitchen, before stepping into the surveillance room on the right.

In here, there were three screens. Each one showed a clear image of the exterior of the house. At the moment, the cameras showed their scenes in real time, but Cole knew how to operate the system. In the past, when he had suspected his fool of a daughter of sneaking out of the house, he had scanned back through an entire night's worth of footage. At high speed, you could do each of the cameras in about five minutes. True, he'd never actually *seen* Izzy trying to escape, but you couldn't be too careful . . .

With the press of a couple of buttons on the small keyboard, he scanned back now. The first screen displayed footage from the camera that covered the front of the house. Staring intently at it, he saw a cat slide backwards across the screen at about 1:30. An hour before that, the enormous front yard seemed to grow a bit lighter for perhaps five minutes – although it was only a few seconds at high speed. He assumed a car had stopped outside and remained stationary with its headlamps on. Aside from that, the front camera had nothing to show him.

He turned his attention to the second screen. This covered one half of the rear garden. For another five minutes, he watched time roll back. But he saw nothing through the constant film of snow, except the snowy ground lighting up at about the time he remembered standing at his office window and looking out over the garden. He could even just make out his own silhouette stretching down from the house. But nothing else.

Camera number three covered the other half of the rear garden. Cole found himself looking at it less closely. Perhaps he'd been mistaken. Perhaps there was a perfectly reasonable explanation for the tracks in the snow. He was probably just on edge, he decided, because of everything that was going to happen today . . .

He gave a low hiss. He had just seen something on the screen.

If Cole had blinked at a different time, he'd have missed it. It was little more than a flicker on the edge of the screen. He stopped the footage then moved it forward frame by frame.

It was a person. He knew that, even though he could not make out a face. All he could see was the person's head drift for less than a second into the camera's field of view. As he paused the footage to examine it, he realized that there must be a blind spot in the garden, a place that the cameras didn't cover. He sneered – there would be hell to pay with the security firm who installed them. But he put that thought to the back of his mind as he studied the image. All he could tell was that the intruder was wearing a baseball cap. The peak was hiding his – or her – face. Above the peak, he could just make out an 'N' and an 'I'.

He stared at the image for a full minute without

moving. What to think? Who *was* this intruder? His eyes narrowed. 'Izzy,' he said under his breath. Because if there was a blind spot in the garden, who would know about it apart from her? She was a dishonest, calculating girl, after all. No doubt she had broken back into the house to find some money. Or persuaded one of her criminal friends to do it for her. It was pathetic, the way she thought she could manage without his generosity. But she couldn't.

Later today, he decided, he would show this footage to the police. They had done precious little to find his daughter so far. He was rather looking forward to gloating that he had furthered their investigation more in a few minutes than they had in a few days. And he felt a sense of relief that this intruder had nothing to do with his business with Dmitri. How could they? It was just a kid.

With a tap of the keyboard, the monitors returned to real time. Cole stood up, brushed himself down and headed to the front door. He would deal with all this when he returned. By that time, he would have handed the suitcase over to the Russians, and he would be a very, very rich man.

18
HAPPY VALLEY

Ricky watched Izzy buy herself a one-day travel card from the busy ticket office at Piccadilly Circus station. She looked anxiously over her shoulder as she passed through the barrier into the underground. Then she disappeared into the crowd of commuters.

Ricky checked his watch. A quarter past eight. He stifled his tiredness. It had been a long night, travelling around London on the night buses, keeping Izzy company as they tried to stay warm. But now he needed his wits about him. He had forty-five minutes to get to the Happy Valley Café in time for Jacob Cole's nine a.m. meeting.

He managed to find a seat on the rush-hour tube. As it trundled towards Kilburn, he pulled his base-ball cap down over his head, closed his eyes and worked out his plan. He knew that Jacob Cole was meeting the Russian, Dmitri. He guessed there might be other Russians there too, and Cole would be handing over the nuclear codes. At the very least, Ricky needed to get a picture of him doing that: proof that Cole was a traitor to his country. And if possible, he needed to snatch the documents before the Russians got their hands on them.

— *So. No pressure. I thought you told Felix that this was a grown-ups' problem.*

— *It is. I'm doing this for Izzy.*

— *For Izzy? Or for Madeleine?*

Ricky frowned under his cap. He didn't like the way the conversation in his head was going. But he did know that he needed to do this; needed to show Felix what he was capable of. And now that he knew what was at stake, he couldn't just walk away.

His feet slapped across the wet, slushy floor of the concourse of Kilburn High Road station. Two ticket collectors were standing by the barriers. He approached them and asked if they knew the way to the Happy Valley Café. One of them shook his head, but the other nodded. 'Right out of the station, turn right at Boots, second on your right.' Ricky thanked them, but they'd already gone back to their conversation.

The street was not nearly as busy as central

London. Ricky turned his baseball cap so that it was pointing backwards, then started tramping along the snowy, slushy pavement towards Boots.

Twenty metres out of the station, he stopped.

Slowly, he turned round.

Was someone following him? It sure felt like it. He scanned the street, but saw nothing except pedestrians walking briskly, their heads down as they went about their business. Then, because he knew better than most that someone who was following you didn't have to be *behind* you, he turned again and looked ahead. He saw nobody suspicious.

– You're just on edge. Nobody's tailing you. Nobody even knows where you are . . .

At Boots, he turned right. There were even fewer people down this side street. And when he came to the second turning on the left, he saw nobody. The Happy Valley Café was about thirty metres along this deserted road.

He drew a deep breath. Then he walked towards the Café.

The Café had a glass frontage. The words 'Happy Valley' were printed in yellow lettering around a picture of an orange sun. Through the glass, Ricky could see that business wasn't brisk. There were only two other people in there – workmen, by the look of their paint-spattered clothes. He reminded himself that it was 27 December. For most people, it was still the Christmas holidays.

The heavy glass door squeaked a bit as Ricky pushed it open. The inside of the Happy Valley Café looked like any other greasy spoon. He counted eight tables, each with four red plastic chairs. On every table there was a red plastic bottle of tomato sauce, a salt cellar and a bottle of vinegar. In an attempt to brighten the place up, each table had a heavy glass vase filled with artificial flowers. But the glass was greasy and the flowers dusty, so they only made the Café look more down-at-heel.

The white tiles on the floor were scuffed and chipped. There was a smell of fat and instant coffee. In front of Ricky, opposite the door, was a serving hatch. A man behind the counter in a blue and white striped apron gave him a welcoming smile as he walked in. He was a jolly-looking guy, rather fat and with a friendly face. His smile looked out of place here, but Ricky couldn't help smiling back at him. From behind the hatch, a radio was blaring loudly – Ricky heard the Capital Radio jingle, then a pop song he didn't recognize.

The workmen were sitting just next to the hatch. Apart from them, Ricky had his choice of tables, so he picked one by the door – if he sat there, he could leave quickly if he needed to. But with his back up against the glass frontage, he also had a view of the whole Café. Wherever Cole and the Russians decided to sit, he would be able to see them.

He tried to look casual as he took a seat. In fact, his eyes were darting around, searching for security cameras. He saw none, and began to understand why Jacob Cole had chosen this place. It was almost empty. Nobody would expect to see him here. And if anyone came asking, he could easily deny it. What would he, an important politician, possibly be doing in a place like this?

But he wouldn't be reckoning on a young kid secretly recording him on his phone. Ricky placed his mobile on the table, then glanced through the smeared, grease-spotted menu. Two minutes later the man from the counter came to take his order.

'Bacon sandwich and a cup of tea, please.' Then he corrected himself. 'Actually, make that a full English.'

The man chuckled. 'You look like you need feeding up, sunshine,' he said.

Ricky nodded, but the truth was that a bigger plate of food would take longer to make and longer to eat. He didn't want to draw attention to himself by sitting in a Café with no food in front of him . . .

He checked the time. 8:55 a.m. He could expect Cole and the Russians to walk in at any moment.

Thirty seconds later, his cup of tea arrived.

And thirty seconds after that, the door opened.

Jacob Cole wore a frown on his thin face. As he stepped inside the café, clutching a leather briefcase in his right hand, he stopped for a moment and glanced around the room. Ricky could tell he hardly registered the boy sitting just two metres away. Cole's eyes lingered for a moment on the workmen sitting by the hatch, and he clearly couldn't help the whisper of a sneer crossing his lips at the sight of their dirty clothes. He crossed the floor of the café and sat at the far end, putting the briefcase in the chair next to him as he picked up the menu. Ricky could tell, though, that he wasn't really reading it – he was just looking over the top of the grease-spattered card, checking out the room.

Ricky picked up his phone and pretended to browse the internet. In reality, he had opened the camera app and set it to video mode. If he held it at an angle just shy of forty-five degrees from the hatch, he had Cole in plain view.

A song Ricky recognized drifted out from behind the hatch as his breakfast arrived. The workmen, who had finished their breakfast, stood up and left. Now it was just Ricky, Cole and the guy behind the counter, who was bringing him his full English.

'Sink your teeth into that, sunshine,' he said.

241

Once Ricky's plate and cup of tea were in front of him, he propped the phone against his hot mug, making sure it was at the correct angle to record Cole and anyone who sat with him. He switched off the camera so that nobody entering the café could tell what he was doing. Then he started on his breakfast.

He was slowly chewing his way through a piece of fried bread – and Cole had ordered himself a coffee in an extremely curt voice – when the door opened again. Two men entered. They were both very broad-shouldered – Ricky's immediate thought was that he wouldn't want to get into a fight with either of them. One of them had jet-black hair, rather scruffy. The other was blond, but his hair was cropped very short. Like Cole, he carried a briefcase, but this one looked a good deal sturdier: it was metallic and seemed rather heavy.

Neither man smiled as they too cast around the room. And just like Cole, they barely seemed to notice Ricky sitting there, concentrating hard on his rasher of bacon.

The two Russians – Ricky knew this must be them – seemed to fill the whole café as they walked towards the table where Jacob Cole was sitting. Izzy's dad, with his thin, mean face, looked tiny compared to them. He spread out his hands to indicate that they should take a seat opposite him. As they sat down, Ricky switched his camera on again and pressed record. He continued with his breakfast, watching the proceedings covertly on the small screen, his ears straining to pick up every word of their hushed conversation.

The blond man spoke first. He had a Russian accent. 'Your suitcase contains the—'

'Yes, Dmitri,' Cole cut in. 'It contains the time-table.'

The Russians chuckled at Cole's coded language. They appeared a lot less tense than him. The black-haired man looked over his shoulder and shouted 'Coffee!' at nobody in particular, and Ricky saw the shadow of a scowl cross the face of the jolly man in the apron. Back at the other side of the café, Cole had placed the briefcase on the table between him and Dmitri.

'Open it,' Dmitri said.

'When I have my money.'

Dmitri smiled. From the inside lapel of his jacket he pulled out a memory stick. 'The funds have been transferred to an untraceable Swiss bank account. You will find the account details, including all the security information you will need, on here.'

Cole eyed the memory stick suspiciously, and took it with obvious reluctance. Ricky had the impression he was expecting cash.

'Now open the briefcase,' Dmitri told him.

Cole gave him a dead-eyed look, then set the numerical code on his briefcase and flicked it open. The file he handed over to the Russian was very slim, but Dmitri handled it as if it was the most precious thing in the world.

'Paper?' Dmitri said. 'How quaint.'

'Paper is safer than electronic files these days,' Cole told him, looking meaningfully at the data stick he had just received. As he closed his briefcase and put it on the floor, Dmitri placed his metallic one on the table, opened it up and deposited the folder inside.

'You'll find that the folder contains a little something else that your people might find useful. Think of it as a free sample. There's plenty more where it came from, but we will, of course, need to discuss a fair price.'

'You're a greedy man,' Dmitri announced. He didn't sound as though he meant it as an insult.

'I just want an honest day's pay for an honest day's work.' Cole's eyes narrowed. 'Tell your people that this new information will be very expensive. But worth it.'

The man arrived with their coffee. He blocked the camera's view of Cole and the Russians, but that didn't matter. Ricky reckoned he had enough. He switched his phone off. The man returned to the serving hatch and Ricky placed some money on his table to pay for his half-eaten breakfast. He wanted to get out of there as quickly as possible.

But something stopped him.

The briefcase was there, sitting on the table. Nobody was holding it. If he was quick, Ricky believed he could snatch it.

– *You're crazy.*

– *Maybe I'm not. That briefcase is the smoking gun. If I have the camera footage and the briefcase, Cole is going to prison for a long time . . .*

He couldn't think too long or too hard about it. If he was going to grab the briefcase, he needed to do it now.

It was almost on instinct that he adjusted his Nike baseball cap so that the peak faced forward and not back. It would shadow his face a little better, he figured. Disguise him.

Big mistake.

Ricky scraped his chair back and stood up, pocketing his phone as he did so. Distance to the briefcase: four metres.

He had covered three metres of it when Cole looked up at him.

Ricky knew, in an instant, that something was

wrong. Cole wasn't staring at his face, but at his baseball cap. Ricky saw him silently mouth the letters 'N' and 'I'.

'*Grab that boy!*' he hissed.

For a big man, Dmitri moved very fast. Before Ricky could even take a step back, the Russian had reached out and seized his wrist. Ricky gasped with pain as Cole stood up and whipped the baseball cap from his head.

Cole stared at the lettering on Ricky's baseball cap, then back at Ricky.

'What's the problem?' Dmitri asked.

'This boy broke into my house last night. It's hardly a coincidence that he's here now.'

Ricky knew that he would remember the seconds that followed for the rest of his life – however long that might be. The jolly guy from behind the counter strode towards them, his face outraged. 'What's going on?' he said. 'What are you doing with that young man? Leave him alone!'

'Stay out of it,' growled Dmitri.

'No I won't. This is my gaff and he's just a kid. Get your bleedin' hands off—'

He never finished his sentence. The dark-haired Russian had turned towards him and Ricky saw that he had a gun in his hand. Without a moment's hesitation, the Russian raised it in the man's direction.

'*No!*' Ricky shouted.

But too late.

The Russian fired.

The shot was very quiet, but its result was deadly. The bullet slammed into the man's forehead and a chunk of his skull the size of Ricky's fist blasted away. A grotesque spatter of blood sprayed over several of the tables as the man slumped to the floor.

There was a sudden, horrible silence. Ricky felt his muscles freeze.

'Gregoriev, you *idiot!*' Cole breathed. 'You . . . you *IDIOT.*'

But Gregoriev wasn't looking at Cole. He had turned his gun on Ricky. The barrel was just half a metre from his face and Ricky could see right down it. He could feel the slight warmth of the metal . . .

Suddenly Cole slammed the Russian's gun arm away. 'For God's sake,' he hissed. Then he turned his fearsome glare on Ricky. Dmitri gripped his wrist even harder and Ricky knew he had only seconds to act, otherwise there was a very good chance he'd be joining the dead man on the floor.

– Remember what Felix told you: 'If you find yourself in a fight with someone, forget all the fancy stuff.

Put your hands on something very heavy and hit them over the head with it.'

Ricky couldn't work out if what he did next was stupid or brave. A bit of both, probably. He stretched his free arm out behind him and grabbed a greasy glass vase from the nearest table. With a great, forceful swing of his arm, he smashed it hard against Dmitri's head.

The vase shattered. Dmitri roared in pain and anger as a huge welt of blood and lacerated skin appeared on his forehead. He let go of Ricky's wrist and clutched his wound. Ricky still had the base of the vase in his hand and its edges were jagged and sharp. He knew he only had one chance to get out of here, so as the second Russian was swinging his gun arm in his direction he hurled the glass at the gunman, who raised both hands to protect himself from the missile.

– *Get out of here! GET OUT OF HERE!*

Cole was pale-faced and frightened. His eyes bulged and Ricky could see that he was about to grab the briefcase from the table. Half of him knew it was foolish to delay, but he grabbed the case before Cole could get it.

Then he turned and got ready to run.

He might have made it if the dirty white tiles on the floor of the café hadn't been covered in blood.

The dead waiter had bled atrociously. He was surrounded by a pool of red, sticky fluid. As Ricky's right foot slapped against the wet floor, he slipped. He tried to balance himself, but it was no good. Still clutching the briefcase, he tumbled to the floor, his legs sprawled over the dead man's hard body. He felt his phone crack in his pocket, but was too scared to consider whether he'd lost the video footage. Right now it only meant one thing: he couldn't call anyone for help.

Sickened with fear, he scrambled to get to his feet again. But it was no good. Already the two burly Russians were standing over him. They didn't care that their boots were spattered with the dead man's blood. Dmitri's face was covered with blood of his own, dripping down the side of his snarling face like a dreadful horror mask where the vase had hit him. And his colleague was there too, his eyes flashing. Both men had guns now, and they were both pointing them directly at Ricky.

There was no escaping. Ricky closed his eyes and waited for the gunshot he knew would end his life.

There was certainly a loud noise. But it wasn't a gunshot, and Ricky wasn't dead. Not yet, at least.

It seemed to happen in slow motion. Ricky heard an ear-splitting crack, then opened his eyes just in time to see the entire glass frontage of the café shatter. With a deafening crash, a million glass shards fell to the floor like icy rain.

In the split second after the explosion, Ricky saw a figure standing outside the café. It was a boy about Ricky's age. He looked weirdly like Ricky himself, with a baseball cap, jeans, a black puffa jacket, a red scarf and black Converse trainers. And in that instant, Ricky knew he had seen him before. Twice. Once in the café in Frith Street. Then later the same evening, fixing his bike outside McDonald's in Shaftesbury Avenue. The boy had a fierce, urgent look in his eyes, and he shouted a single word: '*RUN!*'

Ricky didn't need telling twice. The explosion had forced the two Russians to take a couple of steps backwards. They had raised their arms to cover their faces, so their weapons were no longer pointing at Ricky. He scrambled to his feet, holding the briefcase tightly, and sprinted for the exit. His feet crunched over the broken glass as he ran towards the strange boy, who was pointing to the far end of the street. 'That way!' he urged. '*Go!*'

Ricky had sometimes had a dream where, no matter how fast he ran, he couldn't get to the place he was heading for. He felt like that now. It was only fifty metres to the end of the street, but as the two boys sprinted side by side as hard as they could, it felt to Ricky like they'd never get there.

'We're too close together,' the boy shouted. 'We're an easy target. Split up.'

The advice sounded so much like Felix that Ricky had to glance at the boy to check his eyes hadn't been playing games. '*Who are you?*' Ricky yelled.

But the boy didn't have time to answer. There was the sound of a single gunshot and a bullet flew so close over Ricky's head that he could feel the rush of air as it passed. They were ten metres from the end of the street. 'Turn right!' the boy shouted.

They veered right. Sweat was pouring from Ricky's skin. Breathless, they turned the corner. The boy grabbed him by the arm. 'Give me the briefcase,' he said.

'No way,' Ricky snapped. He didn't know who this kid was, and he certainly wasn't going to surrender his hard-won evidence to him.

The boy didn't argue. Instead, he slapped Ricky on the shoulder. It was a weirdly friendly gesture, given what was happening, but it was hardly the strangest thing that had happened to Ricky that day, so he ignored it. 'Then keep running,' the boy said. 'I'll delay them as long as I can.'

'Who *are* you?' Ricky demanded again, more harshly this time.

The boy had already turned away. 'I'm Zak,' he said. 'Now *go!*'

There was no time to argue. Whoever this boy was, he clearly knew what he was doing. And Ricky had no desire at all to come face to face with those Russians again. His skin still felt clammy from the shock of seeing them kill the man in the café. He looked down and saw the man's blood on his trousers. It made him shudder, but he knew he had no time for squeamishness.

He checked his grip on the suitcase and inhaled deeply.

Then he ran.

19

ALL SOULS

Jacob Cole was trembling with rage and fear.

He had never seen someone killed before. It wasn't like in the movies. He would never forget the sight of that man with half his head blown away. It was this, even more than the fear of the police arriving, that made him sprint after the Russians as they chased the two kids.

Cole might have been a thin man, but he wasn't a fit one. He had a burning sensation in his chest by the time he reached the end of the road. He stood there panting, looking out onto the busier road. Dmitri and Gregoriev were arguing in Russian. They had hidden their weapons, thank God, now that there were more people about, and they were looking left and right, trying to spot those damn kids who were going to ruin everything.

'There!' Cole announced sharply.

He had seen the second boy, who had appeared outside the shattered window. He was on the opposite side of the street, about fifteen metres to their right, sprinting towards a branch of Boots on the corner of the road.

'What about the other one?' Dmitri asked.

He looked very alarming with his bloodied face and Cole could tell that he had violent intentions towards the kid in the Nike baseball cap. But they couldn't get sidetracked: the briefcase was the important thing. If anyone found out what he'd been selling, it wouldn't just be his career that would be at an end. It would be his freedom.

'They were obviously together, you idiot,' Cole snarled. 'Find one and you'll find the other. *Get after him!*'

The Russians burst across the road, forcing a black cab to swerve sharply to avoid hitting them. Cole followed more carefully, but by the time he had reached the opposite pavement, the boy had disappeared. Still gasping for breath, he followed the Russians to the end of the street, where another road ran at right angles. Cole just managed to catch a glimpse of the kid on the other side. He was smiling at them. Then a bus trundled past, blocking him from view.

By the time it had passed, the kid had disappeared.

Cole felt his temperature rising. He wanted to hit someone. He found himself turning a full circle as he searched for the kids, but there was no sign of either of them. It was as if they had vanished into thin air. 'You've lost them!' he shouted accusingly at the Russians. A passer-by gave him a funny look, but he barely noticed. '*FIND THEM!*'

But the two Russians didn't move. They exchanged a grim, purposeful look, then nodded at each other.

'*WHAT ARE YOU WAITING FOR?*' Cole screamed, ignoring the way that even more passers-by were staring at him and keeping their distance. '*I TOLD YOU TO—*'

A brutal punch in the pit of his stomach silenced him – Dmitri was a strong man with a big fist, and it knocked the wind straight out of his lungs. Cole doubled over in pain, gasping desperately for breath but unable to find it. He felt Dmitri grabbing his arm fiercely. The Russian dragged him along the road while Cole coughed and spluttered. He was aware of Gregoriev walking just behind him to his right.

'If you don't want to end up like the guy in the café, keep walking,' Dmitri said under his breath.

Suddenly Cole heard police sirens. He glanced up

ahead to see flashing blue lights coming their way. There was no need to wonder where they were going, and for the briefest moment, Cole considered shouting out. Perhaps he could try to get the attention of the oncoming police. But then he remembered the sight of the dead waiter, bleeding on the floor of the café. He needed to get away from there, before the police decided he was involved with the killing.

And so he staggered along the pavement, Dmitri still gripping his arm, Gregoriev pacing menacingly behind. After thirty metres they took a left turn, then stopped outside a black people-carrier. Cole saw his reflection in the blacked-out windows. He looked gaunt and frightened. There was a beeping sound as Gregoriev pressed a key fob to unlock the vehicle, the side door slid open and Cole felt himself being pushed roughly inside.

Seconds later the door had slammed shut and a clicking sound told Cole it was locked. Dmitri was sitting beside him. He had removed his handgun and was pressing it hard into Cole's ribs. Gregoriev was up front behind the wheel.

'You understand that I'll kill you if you try to escape?' Dmitri said.

Too frightened to reply, Cole nodded vigorously. He thought he might be sick.

Dmitri looked towards Gregoriev. 'You know where to go?'

Gregoriev nodded. From the glove compartment of the car he pulled out what looked like a small sat-nav unit, which he clipped to a bracket on the dashboard and switched on. It took thirty seconds to start up. Cole caught sight of a map with two dots on it. One red, one blue. The blue dot was moving, the red one stationary.

'Go!' Dmitri barked.

Gregoriev turned the ignition key and the engine turned over. The tyres of the people-carrier screeched loudly as the vehicle jolted forward. The barrel of Dmitri's gun jabbed harder into Cole's ribs as it moved.

And the MP realized he had made a horrible mistake . . .

Ricky was running blindly. Questions ricocheted around his head. Who was that strange boy who had just rescued him? He must work for Felix, surely. What was the extra information Cole had given the Russians? Where were they now?

What should he do?

He couldn't answer any of these questions. His only plan was to run. He tried to clear his mind, but the image of the dead body in the Happy Valley

Café kept jumping gruesomely into his mind. Each time he saw that horrible picture in his head he felt nauseous. *It had been his fault.* If he hadn't been recognized, the waiter would not have got involved. He would still be *alive.* The only way he could make good now was to ensure that the man's death had been worthwhile – that the information he carried now got to the right people. To Felix.

But his phone was bust. He had no way of contacting his mentor. So right now, the only thing he could do was run faster and harder as he clutched the heavy briefcase in his increasingly sweaty fist.

Shops, buildings and road junctions passed him by. Ricky didn't know where he was. He ran alongside a children's playground where mums were building a snowman with their kids. Then past a supermarket car park. He stopped to catch his breath in a dank, smelly subway whose walls were covered with graffiti. But he had only taken a few deep breaths when he almost heard Felix's voice cracking like a whip, admonishing him. It would only take his pursuers to come at him from either end of the subway and he'd be trapped. Or if anyone saw him with the briefcase, they'd probably assume he'd nicked it – and it might be worth their while nicking it from *him* . . .

So he kept running.

Many times he almost slipped on the snowy, slushy ground. His shoes and the bottom of his trousers were soaked, but still he kept on going. He could think of nothing but putting as much distance between himself and those terrifying, murderous Russians as possible. And Cole too. Creepy, cowardly, treacherous Cole: Ricky completely got why Izzy never wanted to go home again . . .

Izzy. He pictured her sitting on the tube, waiting for midday. He pictured the police catching up with her and forcing her to go back to her abusive father. And the image of his dead sister Madeleine swam again into his head.

You can't bring your sister back by saving Izzy Cole, you know.

That thought just made Ricky redouble his efforts. Cole and the Russians *couldn't* regain the contents of this suitcase. They *couldn't* catch Ricky and stop him from bringing them to justice . . .

He had been running for twenty-five minutes and his energy was spent. He stopped suddenly, his body doubled over as he gasped for breath. Only after thirty seconds of inhaling deeply did he look around.

He was outside an old church whose stones were black from pollution. The church sat alongside a busy road, but there were very few pedestrians here.

Even so, Ricky felt conspicuous. A panel on the railing surrounding the entrance said: 'The Church of All Souls, Harlesden'.

– Don't just stand in the middle of the pavement where anybody can see you. Conceal yourself!

The voice in his head was giving him good advice. Ricky's eyes fell on the heavy wooden door of the church. He approached it and tried the iron handle. To his surprise, it twisted open. He stepped into the church. His foster parents had put him off churches, but this one looked like the normal everyday sort, not the kind they had dragged him along to.

It was several degrees colder inside. Ricky stood at the entrance looking around to see if there was any-body in here. It appeared to be deserted. A bright winter sun was shining through the stained glass behind the altar up ahead and the light dazzled him slightly so he moved to the shade at the side of the church.

– You need an exit strategy.

He looked at the far end of the church. There was a door behind the altar and Ricky could see that it was ajar. If a threat entered through the main door, he could leave by the rear.

He sat down next to a bookcase full of prayer books. Here, he placed the briefcase on his lap. He had not seen Dmitri lock the case, so he wasn't surprised when it clicked open.

Ricky found that his hands were trembling as he removed the manila folder from inside.

He winced. From somewhere in the church there was a very quiet, high-pitched whine. Like electrical interference, but very faint. He looked around quickly, double-checking that there was nobody here. But no, the place *seemed* deserted. Where was the noise coming from? The altar, perhaps?

Or maybe he was imagining it. The noise was extremely faint, and when he concentrated on it, it seemed to fade away.

He turned his attention back to the folder. His hands still shaking slightly, he opened it.

20

TRACKED

There were only four sheets of paper inside. The first was headed:

Security Clearance 1
Trident Nuclear Deterrent
Location Codes

The rest of the page was filled with sequences of numbers that meant nothing to Ricky. But he knew that in the wrong hands, this single piece of paper could spell disaster.

Felix's voice rang in his head. *Have you ever heard the phrase 'nuclear winter'?* Ricky shuddered. It was frightening to think that such an innocent-looking piece of paper had the potential to cause so much horror. He found himself automatically memorizing the codes.

He put it to one side, and looked at the next document in the folder. This was completely different. Stapled to the top of the sheet was a passport photograph of a man with a friendly, open face and dark, scruffy hair. His name, according to the attached document, was Alistair Bishop. But the document explained that he had other names too: James Marshall, Raymond Carrick, Thomas Parker . . .

Ricky's mind flashed back to his first meeting with Felix. What was it Felix had said? *Names. Some are more suitable than others for different occasions.* Back then, Ricky had assumed that someone with lots of different names would be a criminal. Now it seemed more likely that they were part of the secret world. Like Felix. Like Zak, the boy who had just saved him.

Like Ricky himself.

Ricky read on. The first main paragraph of the document told him exactly who Alistair Bishop was:

Bishop is currently Moscow correspondent for The Times. *This is deep cover. He is an MI6 operative with excellent access to several high-level Russian ministers. In the past twelve months he has forwarded large quantities of classified intelligence which MI6 consider to be of especially high quality.*

Ricky blinked. He knew very little about the

secret world, but he knew this: if the likes of Dmitri found out that this guy was a British spy, it would end *very* badly for him.

He looked through the remaining documents. They contained the details of three more British agents. There was a Russian national high up in the Russian navy. There was a female aid worker in the Ukraine. And finally an English teacher at a school in St Petersburg where wealthy and influential Russians sent their children . . .

– *You understand what this is, right? Cole is selling the details of British agents working undercover abroad. If Dmitri and his friend get their hands on this information, these people are as good as dead.*

– *And Cole said there was plenty more where these came from . . .*

Ricky felt his lip curling with distaste.

Suddenly he winced again. That high-pitched whining had returned. Or maybe it had been there all along, and Ricky had zoned it out. He looked around again. There was definitely nobody else in the church. So where was it coming from?

– *Don't worry about it. It's nothing. You need to think what you're going to do next.*

Ricky looked at the documents in his hands. Perhaps he should destroy them now. That way the Russians could never get their hands on them. But something stopped him. If he destroyed the documents, he would destroy the hard evidence he had against Cole. He thought of Izzy, so terrified of her abusive father that she could never go home.

His lip curled again. He wasn't going to let Cole get away with this. No way.

He placed the documents back in the metal briefcase. Then he clicked it shut.

His eyes narrowed. The whining sound had stopped.

A new tendril of fear unravelled itself in Ricky's gut. He slowly opened the briefcase again. The whining sound returned.

It felt as though Ricky was moving in slow motion. He took the folder out of the briefcase and laid it on the pew next to him. Then he examined the briefcase a little more closely.

It took about ten seconds for him to realize that the briefcase had a false base. He managed to worm his fingers round the edges and detach it.

The sight of what lay below made his breath catch in his throat. There was a mess of loose wires: brown, blue and yellow. They were connected to a circuit board and to a small battery cell with two AA batteries. For a horrible moment, Ricky thought he was looking at an explosive device. But then his eyes picked out a small chip soldered to the circuit board.

In narrow white lettering it contained the letters: GPS.

Ricky touched the mess of wires. The whining sound stopped. There was clearly a loose connection somewhere. If there hadn't been, he would never have known that the suitcase contained what was, quite obviously, a tracking device.

And if there was a tracking device, it meant there was someone tracking him.

The Russians.

– Get the batteries out. Quickly! Disable it!

As soon as that thought rebounded in his head, he heard the screeching of tyres outside and he felt a surge of adrenalin.

– They're here! THEY'VE FOUND YOU!

Ricky's fingers felt suddenly clumsy as he fumbled to remove the batteries from the cell. Once they were out, he shoved them in his pocket and replaced the false base. He slammed the briefcase shut, then grabbed the folder. Removing his rucksack from his back, he crammed the documents inside. His fingers touched the jewellery he had stolen from Izzy's house the night before, but right now he wasn't thinking about diamonds. He slung the rucksack over his shoulder again, grabbed the briefcase and sprinted up the aisle.

– Put the briefcase on top of the altar. When they see

it, they'll stop to look inside. It'll give you a few extra seconds.

Ricky did as the voice in his head told him. However, as he laid the briefcase on the altar, he heard voices outside. They were shouting in Russian. He had barely taken two steps away from the altar when the heavy door of the church swung open. Dmitri and Gregoriev appeared. They took one look at Ricky and sprinted up the aisle towards him, their heavy boots echoing around the church as they ran.

Ricky sprinted for the door behind the altar and slipped through it. It led into a dark, poky vestry, and to his horror there was no external door – just a small window that couldn't be opened. Frosted glass, wooden frame with peeling paint. Ricky spun round and examined the door. There was an internal bolt, which meant he could lock himself into this little room. He quickly engaged the bolt – just in time, because a second later he heard the heavy thumping of a fist against the door itself.

But now he was stuck inside, sweating and panicking . . .

– Think. Think!

Ricky took in the contents of the room with a single glance. Along one wall was a line of priest's cassocks, and along the opposite wall was another bookcase full of prayer books.

He needed to hide the documents. It was only a matter of time before the Russians broke their way into the vestry. Minutes, if he was lucky. More likely seconds. He quickly strode up to the bookcase and removed a prayer book. Opening it up, he ripped out clumps of pages from the middle . . .

There was a sudden thump on the door. It rattled alarmingly in the door frame. Ricky could picture either Dmitri or his mate shoulder-barging the door.

– It's not going to hold!

Ricky lowered his rucksack and shoved his hand inside. He pulled out the documents, folded them twice and then placed them in the cavity he had created in the hymn book.

There was another colossal crash against the door. The iron latch shuddered.

– You've got less than thirty seconds!

Ricky hesitated for a moment. Then he dug inside his rucksack for a second time and pulled out Izzy's mum's jewellery. He placed this inside the hymn book along with the documents, then carefully returned the doctored book to the shelf. He took a split second to satisfy himself that the damaged book looked no different to the others, then he took the ripped-up pages and shoved them inside the pocket of the dustiest, least-used cassock he could find. There was a pen inside the cassock. Instinctively, Ricky pocketed it for himself.

Thud!

An alarming creaking sound accompanied the third shoulder-barge on the door. One more, maybe two, and the Russians would be in here.

Ricky grabbed another prayer book from a different shelf. Then he turned his attention to the window.

It was about two metres off the ground. In size, a metre square. Ricky reckoned he could climb through it, but he needed to shatter the glass first. He pushed the table up to the wall and lifted the heavy chair onto it.

Thud!

Glancing over his shoulder, Ricky could see that the bolt was splintering away from the door frame. He jumped onto the table, then awkwardly lifted the chair and slammed it feet first against the window.

The glass held.

He slammed again.

Nothing.

Thud!

The bolt splintered inwards. The door was a couple of centimetres ajar.

— It'll only take one more hit!

For the third time, Ricky slammed the chair against the glass, putting behind it all the strength his exhausted body could muster.

Finally, it gave way.

For the second time that morning, the sound of shattering glass filled his ears. Ricky threw the chair back towards the door – one more obstacle to slow the Russians down. There was still some jagged glass around the window frame, so he used his sleeve to force it away, then winced as a shard of glass sliced into the back of his hand. It started bleeding badly, but he couldn't let that slow him down. Clutching the prayer book and the pen, he practically hurled himself through the open window, falling heavily on the hard ground outside.

He winced as his knees and ankles jarred, then collapsed into a heap.

Half a metre away from where he was standing, he saw a pair of feet.

He looked up.

Jacob Cole was staring down at him.

Cole's face was twisted with anger. There was a mad fire in his eyes, his grey hair was dishevelled and a vein pumped in his neck. He took a threatening step towards Ricky.

Two steps.

Ricky heard a clattering on the other side of the open window, and he knew the Russians had got into the vestry. He looked around. He was in a cobbled alleyway along the end of the church. High above him was the stained-glass window he'd seen from inside. The only way out was along the alleyway, which meant getting past Cole.

Ricky held the pen in his good hand, the prayer book in his bleeding one. He pushed himself up to his feet.

Cole sneered nastily. 'I won't be giving autographs today,' he said. 'And I really think it's a bit late for prayers, don't you, you stupid little boy?'

Ricky looked at the prayer book. 'Actually,' he said, 'I don't.'

He moved quickly. With a sudden, sharp gesture he whacked the sturdy spine of the prayer book hard against Cole's neck. Cole made a pained, strangled sound, then staggered uncertainly. But Ricky wasn't finished with him yet. With a brutal swipe of his arm, he stabbed the pen hard into Cole's right thigh. It punctured his trousers and sank deep into his flesh.

Cole howled in agony. Ricky left the pen sticking out of his leg, then jumped to his feet. 'That's for Izzy,' he hissed, before pushing his open palm hard against Cole's face and knocking him out of the way.

He glanced back. Dmitri was already climbing out of the broken window.

– *Run.*

The voice in his head was more urgent than it had ever been.

– *Run! Run! Run!*

Ricky skittlered down the alleyway. He knew he had to find reserves of energy and speed from somewhere, and somehow he did. He ignored the blood flowing from his hand as he flew across the cobblestones. The open end of the alleyway was thirty metres away. He looked back over his shoulder to see Dmitri the same distance behind him. The welt that Ricky had inflicted on the Russian's face looked even worse than before, but Dmitri wasn't running after him. Instead he had pulled out his gun and was cocking it.

Ricky sprinted even faster. Twenty metres to the exit. His skin tingled. He knew the gunshot was coming soon. Pictures flashed into his mind of the horrific, fatal wound the Russians had inflicted on the guy in the café.

– *Swerve! It'll make you a more difficult target!*

He veered left and right. Fifteen metres to the exit.

Gunshot!

He knew exactly where the bullet had hit. On the

wall, just to his left. It ricocheted off at an angle just in front of him, sending a cloud of powdered brick up into the air. Some of the debris smarted against his face, and he winced. But he kept moving forward, still swerving as he went, putting as much distance between himself and the gunman as he could.

Ten metres to the exit.

His muscles burned.

Five metres.

– *Look out!*

Suddenly the opening to the alleyway was blocked. Gregoriev was there. The huge bulk of his body seemed to fill the exit, and he was holding the metallic briefcase flat out in front of him. Although Ricky tried to swerve past him he knew, without question, that he'd never manage it.

Two seconds later he collided with the briefcase. It was like hitting a brick wall. Ricky felt the wind knocked from his lungs as he smashed into the sturdy metal. Then he shouted out in pain. The Russian had grabbed him by his bleeding hand. Now he had his other immense fist round Ricky's neck and was squeezing so hard that Ricky felt his knees collapsing beneath him.

He struggled and writhed, trying to get away, but it was no good. The Russian had him.

And then the others were there – Dmitri and Cole. Ricky felt a sudden, heavy boot in his guts and a nasty, choking, coughing sound erupted from his throat.

He heard Cole's thin, weasly voice. 'What are we going to do with him?'

Another boot in the pit of his stomach. Ricky saw stars.

Dmitri's voice. A low, angry rumble. 'First,' he said, 'we're going to find out who put him up to this. Then we're going to take back what we've paid for.'

'What then?' Cole hissed.

'Then,' said the Russian, 'we're going to kill him.'

21

FLASHBANG

Ricky had never known fear like it.

The two Russians had him, one on either side, gripping him hard around the elbow. Ricky struggled and writhed as they dragged him along the side of the church. Cole was limping alongside them. He had removed the pen from his leg, but had lost none of the anger in his eyes.

Ricky racked his brains, trying to remember anything Felix had taught him that might be helpful in a situation like this. But none of his training had covered how to escape from two brutal thugs hellbent on killing you. So he did the only thing that came to mind: he yelled.

'Help! *Help me!*'

'Shut him up,' growled Dmitri. A split second later Ricky felt a fist connect violently with his stomach. He doubled over, gasping and spluttering. He wouldn't be trying that again.

They turned a corner and Ricky saw that they were at the front of the church again. There was a black people-carrier parked outside and the Russians dragged him towards it. In a matter of seconds he was inside and Dmitri had him pinned down in the back, a handgun digging sharply into his guts. Cole and Gregoriev were up front. The people-carrier screeched away. Nobody spoke. Sweat poured from Ricky's clammy body almost as fast as the blood from his wounded hand. Half of him wanted to continue struggling. The other half knew that Dmitri would like nothing more than to slam a bullet into his guts.

As they drove, the only sound came from Cole. His leg was obviously bothering him, and he kept muttering to himself – a low, unpleasant hiss, like a wounded snake. Ricky barely noticed where they were travelling. From the corner of his eye he saw a busy grey flyover and a signpost for the M1. He half registered a Big Yellow Storage Company, then twigged that they were in some faceless industrial estate.

The people-carrier screeched to a halt outside some kind of big grey warehouse. A large white shutter covered the vehicle entrance. Dmitri held up a key fob, pressed a button and it automatically opened. It closed again once the vehicle was inside the warehouse.

Total darkness. As Dmitri dragged Ricky out of the vehicle, the sound of the door slamming shut echoed for a good five seconds, making him realize that this was a big building. He felt himself being pressed violently down to his knees. The two Russians said something in their native language and a few seconds later a massive overhead strip light switched on. It was accompanied by an electric humming sound, just on the edge of Ricky's hearing.

Ricky saw that he was indeed in a massive warehouse. Stone floor. Iron rafters in the ceiling. He looked around for an exit strategy. There was a fire door at the far end of the warehouse, but it was heavily padlocked. In any case, if Ricky made a run for it, they'd shoot him down before he even went ten paces.

Apart from that one door and the electric vehicle entrance, there was no means of escape.

Dmitri stood over him. He had his gun pointing directly at his head. Not so close, though, that Ricky could reach out and grab the weapon. It struck him that Dmitri had done this sort of thing before.

Gregoriev approached, his footsteps echoing in

the cavernous space. Ricky felt his strong hands patting him down. He located Ricky's phone, pulled it out then dropped it on the floor and ground it into pieces with his heel.

– *The video evidence! It's gone!*

But Ricky had more important things to worry about than his destroyed footage.

'Hand over the documents,' Dmitri demanded.

'I don't have them,' Ricky whispered. His voice was hoarse, and after the kickings he'd received, it hurt to speak.

Wrong answer. Dmitri's knee cracked against the side of Ricky's face. He felt his cheekbone go and a spurt of blood spray from his nose.

'HAND OVER THE DOCUMENTS!'

'*I . . . don't . . . have . . . them . . .*' Ricky gasped.

Dmitri barked something in Russian and Gregoriev strode over and roughly yanked the rucksack off Ricky's back. As Ricky cringed on the floor in pain, the Russian turned the rucksack inside out to empty its contents over the floor.

Two items fell out. The first was the photograph of Ricky and his parents. The corner of the frame smashed against the hard floor. The letter from Madeleine followed. It settled on the ground next to the picture. The Russian grabbed it and pulled the letter from the envelope, clearly looking to see if

Ricky had hidden the documents in there. When he saw it was just a letter, he screwed it up and threw it to the ground.

'No!' Ricky tried to shout, but his voice was weak and hoarse.

Suddenly Cole was there, crouching down beside Ricky, his lip curled in fury. There was a patch of blood on his trousers where the pen had entered. 'What have you done with those papers, you little—'

But Dmitri knocked Cole violently aside. He bent down and pulled Ricky up by his shoulders. Then he dragged him to the people-carrier and pressed him up against the side of the vehicle. Although his Russian accent was very strong, his English was excellent. He spoke slowly and very precisely so that Ricky could hear every word.

'Understand this. You *will* tell me where those documents are. Either you do it freely, or we do it the other way. But believe me when I tell you, if we do it the other way, you will be begging to tell me where they are, and then you will be begging me to kill you. Now I'm going to ask you this question only once. *Where are the documents?*'

The question seemed to hang in the air between them and Ricky's mind raced. He tried to put the pain of his bruised and bleeding body out of his head. To think straight. To make the right call.

It was impossible.

The world was spinning. His whole body was infused with a mixture of terror and pain. He looked across the warehouse and saw Izzy's dad staring angrily at him. Suddenly Cole's face seemed to change and he saw Izzy herself.

He knew it wasn't really her. He knew his mind was playing tricks on him. But the image of Izzy gave him an encouraging smile. That smile, in turn, gave him a little bit of strength.

He heard himself speaking. 'I don't know where they are—'

Sudden, acute pain. Dmitri had thumped his fist against Ricky's damaged cheekbone. He heard himself howling in agony and the world spun twice as fast. Nausea coursed through his body. He looked towards the image he had seen of Izzy Cole.

But she had changed . . .

It was very subtle, because Izzy and Madeleine looked so alike. But amid the confusion, the fear and the pain, Ricky could see his sister's face, as clearly as if she was really alive.

He knew it was just an apparition, but it gave him some sort of strength. The easy thing would be to give up. But the consequences would be devastating. The Trident codes would be in the wrong hands. Four British agents would be as good as dead. And Jacob Cole would walk free, ready to bully and terrorize anyone and everyone as he saw fit.

What would Ricky's sister think of him, if he allowed that to happen? If he thought only of himself, when there were more important things at stake?

– *So Felix was right. 'One day you might surprise yourself...'*

And then the world stopped spinning. Cole was Cole again. Everything was clear. Ricky looked Dmitri straight in the eye. 'You might as well kill me now,' he said, 'because I'm not going to tell you where they are.'

For a fraction of a second, Ricky saw a tiny shadow of doubt on Dmitri's face. But it passed just as quickly. Dmitri grabbed a clump of his hair, yanked it forward and pushed Ricky down onto the floor yet again. He felt a heavy boot in the small of his back. Then he heard a noise he had learned to recognize: the dull clunking sound of Gregoriev cocking his handgun.

'Wait!'

It was Dmitri who had spoken. He was talking English – Ricky realized that was for Cole's benefit, not Ricky's.

'What's that on his back?'

Ricky didn't know what he was talking about. There was nothing on his back – not even his ruck-sack, which was lying in a heap several metres away from him.

He sensed Dmitri leaning over, then felt the Russian's hand on his left shoulder.

He remembered something. The boy who had rescued him from the Happy Valley Café – Zak, was it? – had given him a friendly slap on that left shoulder just before they split. Ricky had thought it was weird at the time, but maybe . . .

He looked up. Dmitri was holding something. It was very small. Ricky would have confused it with one of those tiny, disc-shaped batteries if it hadn't had a hook-shaped wire protruding from the centre. Dmitri held it up higher, as if examining a precious gemstone.

Then he said: 'Someone is tracking us. Get out of here! *Get out!*'

But too late. Half a second later, the strip lighting overhead failed. The electric humming fell silent.

Total darkness.

There was a clattering of footsteps. He sensed that Cole and one of the Russians were running through the darkness towards the people-carrier. The second Russian – Ricky thought it was Dmitri – bent over to grab him by the scruff of his neck and pull him violently up to his feet . . .

A sudden explosion ripped through the ware-house. It didn't come from the vehicle entrance Ricky and the Russians had used, but from the locked door at the opposite end. By chance, Ricky was facing that way. He saw a sudden orange flash as the door blasted inwards. In the middle of that flash was the silhouette of a person. Ricky couldn't tell anything about them – whether they were male or female, young or old – but in that brief moment of vision he could tell this: the newcomer was armed. It looked to Ricky's untutored eye like they were holding an assault rifle.

A moment later, the blast from the explosion knocked both Ricky and Dmitri back. The Russian lost hold of him as a cloud of dust and debris rained down on them. Ricky rolled away from his kidnapper, wincing as his bleeding hand pressed against something sharp on the ground. In the few seconds since the lights had gone out, Ricky's eyes had grown slightly more used to the darkness. He could see the outline of Dmitri. He was down on one knee, gun arm outstretched, getting ready to fire.

It was another of those moments that was either very brave or very stupid. Ricky hurled himself at the Russian and collided sharply with his body, knocking him over before he could fire.

Just as their two bodies collided, Ricky heard a woman's voice from the doorway. '*Flashbang!*' she shouted.

Suddenly there was a second explosion – a huge cracking sound that split through the air and was like a spike in Ricky's eardrums. A blinding flash accompanied it, as if a vast flash of lightning had struck inside the warehouse itself. Ricky was blinded, deafened and disorientated. He rolled away from Dmitri, clutching his head, trying to shake away the confusion. He needed to get out of there, but he wasn't even sure he could stand up . . .

Footsteps. There was more than one person entering the room.

Ricky's head was spinning. He needed to get to his feet. To get out of there . . .

A voice shouted: '*Stay down!*' Ricky recognized it. It was the boy called Zak.

He hugged the floor, just as two gunshots rang out. They came from two different weapons – Ricky saw a spark from each one as they fired. And again, behind each spark, and despite his dazzled eyes, he could just make out the outline of a figure.

The two Russians started to scream. They'd been hit. Ricky kept low, his sight and senses gradually recovering. One of the figures ran right past him, and Ricky thought he could see that they were wearing some kind of headgear. He remembered Felix talking about night-vision goggles that allowed you to see in the dark. These figures were moving around as easily as if it was broad daylight. That had to be what they were wearing . . .

The woman's voice again. 'Cole! Get on the ground with your hands on your head, otherwise I shoot!'

Cole whimpered pathetically, and there was a scuffling sound. He was clearly doing exactly what he was told. The Russians were still howling with pain, and Ricky himself was feeling more than a little panicked. Who were these people? Friends? Enemies? Neither?

'What's happening?' he yelled through the chaos. *What the hell's happening?*

The overhead light returned. Ricky squinted painfully.

Then he looked round.

22

ALONE AGAIN

He had been right. There were three newcomers in the warehouse.

The first was a boy about Ricky's age. To start with, Ricky couldn't quite make out his features as he was indeed wearing night-vision goggles. So far as Ricky could tell he wasn't armed, but that didn't seem to bother him. He had Cole flat out on the ground, one arm bent up behind his back. In a single, deft move, he took a white plastic cable tie from his pocket and used this to bind Cole's wrists tightly behind his back. Then he himself stood up and raised his goggles and Ricky saw that it was Zak.

Ricky zoned in on his companions. There was a man and a woman. They were also both removing their night-vision goggles. Ricky had seen the man before, with Zak at the café in Frith Street. He had blond hair and a grim, serious face. He was stowing the handgun into a holster strapped to his body. The woman had shoulder-length white-blonde hair. She too was familiar. Had he seen her when he'd stormed out of the apartment? She clearly felt the need to hold onto her gun as she walked up to the whimpering Dmitri.

Dmitri and his friend were bleeding heavily from their shoulders. They had clearly both been shot in the same place, and Ricky realized that this was exactly what the newcomers had wanted. They were sharp shooters, no question. The woman didn't look too concerned by their dramatic-looking wounds, however. 'You'll live, sweetie,' she told the Russian. 'More's the pity.' She looked over at Ricky. 'Hurt, Ricky?' she asked him.

Ricky looked at his bleeding hand. 'It's . . . it's nothing,' he managed to say.

– *She knows your name. She must be something to do with Felix . . .*

'Good.'

As she spoke, Dmitri had shuffled along the floor to where his handgun was lying and was reaching out to grab it. Ricky was about to scream 'Look out!' but he didn't need to. The woman spun round, almost like a ballet dancer, and cracked her foot hard against Dmitri's wrist. The Russian screamed again, but nobody paid him any attention. The woman picked up the loose gun and removed the magazine. The blond man did the same with Gregoriev's gun. Then they tied the Russians' hands behind their backs, just as Zak had done with Cole's, ignoring their howls of pain and their bleeding shoulders as they did so.

While all this was happening, Ricky's eyes darted around the warehouse.

– How did the lights turn on and off?

– Somebody must be operating the fuse board.

Which meant there had to be a fourth person.

Ricky looked towards the blasted-open door just in time to see Felix walk in.

Felix took in the scene of devastation with a single sweep of his head. Then his eyes fell on Ricky. He limped up to his former pupil, then held out one hand to help him up. But Ricky didn't need his help. He struggled to his feet by himself.

'Nice work, Coco,' Felix said quietly.

Ricky looked over at the remains of his mobile phone, which Dmitri had crushed with his heel. 'I had footage of Cole handing the code over to the Russians. I guess that's the end of that.'

Felix strode over to the crushed phone and carefully picked up all the pieces. He carried them carefully back to Ricky. 'You'll be amazed at what we can retrieve from a damaged hard drive. My guess is that Jacob Cole is going to prison for a very long time. Thanks to you.'

'I did it for Izzy,' he said.

'You did it by disobeying every rule in the book. But nice work, all the same.'

Ricky glanced across the room. The woman with the white-blonde hair was forcing the wounded Russians towards the people-carrier, where Cole had collapsed to his knees and had his head bowed.

'Next time, though,' Felix added, 'maybe you should let people know what you're doing. That was kind of close.'

'There isn't going to be a next time,' Ricky said. 'I don't know if you noticed, but I'm lucky to be alive. Which is more than you can say for this guy in the café where they met.' He felt himself trembling as he remembered the horror of that moment. 'They killed him,' he said hotly. 'They put a gun to his head and *killed* him.'

'I know,' Felix said, 'and I'm sorry you had to see that. But maybe there are people out there who you'll stop meeting the same fate, if you complete your training.'

'I'm just a kid,' Ricky hissed.

Felix shook his head. 'You haven't been a kid for a long time, Ricky.'

Before Ricky could respond, Zak walked up to them. He had picked up Ricky's rucksack, along with the picture and the letter. 'Yours?' he asked.

'Thanks,' Ricky muttered, accepting them.

'I see you've met Agent 21,' Felix said.

Ricky blinked. So *this* was the guy Felix had talked about.

'Do you slap a tracking device on the shoulder of everyone you meet?' Ricky asked. He knew he didn't sound too friendly.

'Only the ones I think might end up dead if I don't,' said Zak.

There was no time to reply. Suddenly, from somewhere in the distance outside the warehouse, came the sound of sirens. Police. Ricky, Felix, Zak and his two companions all turned to look at the vehicle entrance.

'I'll deal with them,' Felix said. He turned to Ricky. 'Well, I guess this is goodbye.'

'I guess it is.'

'I've one favour to ask. The codes – are they somewhere safe?'

Ricky nodded.

'Go with Agent 21. Retrieve them and give them to him.'

Ricky couldn't see a problem with that. He nodded again. And without looking back, he headed towards the door that just a few moments ago had been blasted in. Zak caught up with him, and together they left the warehouse.

They walked in silence round to the front of the warehouse. The sirens were much louder now, and Ricky suddenly saw two police cars screaming down the road of the industrial estate towards them.

'Just keep walking in the opposite direction,' Zak said. 'They never notice kids like us. It's like we're invisible.'

'Yeah,' Ricky said bitterly. 'I guess that's what makes us so valuable.'

Zak gave a half-smile, but said nothing.

'You'd been following me, hadn't you? I saw you fixing your bike outside McDonald's.'

'Well spotted,' Zak said. 'Most people wouldn't have noticed. Felix must have been teaching you well.'

'I'm sure he'd like to think so.'

That smile again. It put Ricky on edge.

'Who are the others?' he asked. 'The blonde woman and the guy?'

'They're my Guardian Angels,' Zak said. 'Like Felix is yours. We all have them. Their names are Raf and Gabs. Thanks to them, I'm still alive. I learn everything I can from them. I find I live longer that way.' He paused. 'But that doesn't mean I always have to do what they say. Where are we going, by the way?'

'All Souls Church, Harlesden,' Ricky said. And he picked up his pace to indicate that he didn't want to talk any more.

It took ten minutes to find a taxi, and another ten to get to the church where Cole and the Russians had caught him. It was still deserted. They entered by the front gate and their footsteps echoed as they walked up the aisle towards the altar, then into the vestry behind, its door wide open. The ironmongery and timber on the inside was damaged where the Russians had forced it open. The table was still by the broken window, and the chair was on its side on the floor.

Zak looked around the room in silence. He seemed kind of impressed.

Ricky headed over to the shelf of prayer books. He picked out the book that he'd doctored, and was relieved that the documents were still there, as was the precious necklace he had stolen from Izzy's mum.

He laid the items out on the table, then checked through the documents to make sure they were all there. 'Cole was selling something else to the Russians,' Ricky said. 'Not just the codes. He was offering them the details of British agents across the world. I figured that wouldn't be good.'

Zak looked at the documents. 'You figured right,' he said quietly. 'You've saved a lot of lives today, Ricky. If an agent's cover is blown without him or her knowing it, their life is immediately in danger. That could have been me.' He gave Ricky a piercing look. 'Or you.'

Ricky couldn't hold his gaze for long. He looked back down at the table and picked up the diamond necklace.

'Flashy,' Zak said. 'Want to tell me what it is?'

'I stole it from Jacob Cole's house,' Ricky said. He jutted out his chin. 'I suppose you're going to tell me to give it back.'

'I'm not going to tell you to do anything,' said Zak.

There was a silence. Ricky had a question on the tip of his tongue, but something was holding him back.

– *Ask him.*

– *What's the point? It's all over now. I'm not joining them.*

– *You're being childish. Just ask him.*

'Did Felix tell you why I walked away?' Ricky said finally.

Zak nodded. 'You didn't want to give up Izzy Cole's location.'

'Felix would have done it,' Ricky said hotly. 'He'd

have sent her back to live with a father who beat her up. I wasn't going to let that happen.'

'And you didn't.' Zak seemed perfectly calm. It rather took the wind out of Ricky's sails. They stood in silence again. This time it was broken by Zak. 'In our line of work,' he said, 'you're told to do things. *How* you do them is up to you. My advice is to listen to your Guardian Angel. Learn everything you can from him. But don't stop thinking for yourself, because the moment you do that . . .' His voice trailed away and he looked meaningfully at the necklace on the table. 'You could be a great agent, Ricky. Do some good in the world. Or you can carry on as a thief. The choice is yours.'

'You don't understand anything,' Ricky spat. 'If I sell that necklace, I can stay safe for several months. Safe from adults. Safe from the street. Safe from all this . . .' He waved his arm around the vestry to indicate the broken window.

'I understand more than you think,' said Zak. He picked up the documents from the table and stowed them in his jacket. 'I thought you were OK. Maybe I was wrong.' He walked towards the vestry door, but before he left he stopped and turned back to Ricky. 'I wonder what your parents would say,' he said.

'My parents are dead,' Ricky spat.

Zak smiled sadly. 'Mine too. I decided to grow up

after it happened. What did you decide?' Without waiting for an answer, he quietly walked through the damaged vestry door and disappeared into the church.

Ricky listened to his footsteps fade and disappear. He grabbed the necklace and shoved it in his pocket. And then, because he had decided he didn't want to come face to face with Agent 21 again, he climbed back out through the broken window.

Alone again.

23

SOMETHING GOOD AND CLEVER

Midday.

Izzy Cole stepped out onto the concourse at Piccadilly Circus. She looked towards the newspaper kiosk opposite the exit to Regent Street. Her sharp eyes tried to pick out Ricky. There was no sign of him at first. Everyone she saw milling around the kiosk was an adult.

But wait. Who was that? There was someone with their back to him, and it looked like a boy. He was handing over some money for a newspaper. Izzy walked fast towards him. He turned and she stopped. It wasn't Ricky. The boy disappeared into the crowd. And although it was very busy, Izzy suddenly felt quite alone again.

Five minutes passed. Ten. No sign of him. Izzy reminded herself of what Ricky had said. *If I miss our meeting, then we'll turn up at the same place, same time the following day.*

She felt foolish believing him. Ricky had let her down. She supposed she had better get used to it. Because she had learned one thing: in the end, *everybody* lets you down.

She wouldn't be returning tomorrow. No way. She'd had enough of relying on other people. She was on her own now.

Izzy turned away from the kiosk and started walking, though she didn't quite know where to. All she knew was that she *wasn't* going home. She would have to spend the night on the street again. She had barely any money, and the only other option she could think of was Hunter's. And if she went there, she'd lose everything.

At the last minute, she looked back over her shoulder, a tiny part of her expecting to see Ricky – late and flustered, but there at last.

He wasn't, so she left.

It was mid-afternoon.

Ricky's hand throbbed. He had bought disinfectant and bandages from a chemist. In a filthy alleyway he had poured the disinfectant over the cut on his hand, wincing as it stung his damaged flesh. He had bound it tightly, but already the clean bandage looked grubby. He would have to buy more medical supplies, but his money was running low – he only had ten pounds left in the world. And there was no way he could pickpocket anybody with his hand like this. Too clumsy. He'd be caught in an instant.

He walked up Kingsway, away from Holborn station. It had started snowing again, and all the other pedestrians had their heads down and their hands deep in their pockets. Not Ricky. He walked against the tide, snow settling on his hair and shoulders. And although his good hand was in his pocket, it wasn't to keep it warm. It was to reassure himself that the necklace he had stolen from Mrs Cole – the only thing of any financial value that he owned – was still there.

After 300 metres, he turned right into Chancery Lane. There were far fewer people here, but out of habit Ricky stopped and looked carefully around. There was no sign of a tail. No Zak. No Felix. No nobody. He was almost sure he was alone and unobserved. But then, he told himself, he'd thought that before.

He continued for 200 metres along Chancery Lane, before crossing a road and taking a side street on the left. Moments later he was standing outside a doorway. A painted wooden plaque read:

'F. S. Randolph, Jeweller'. Randolph was definitely the name of the guy Tommy had said was willing to buy stolen jewellery.

– *So you've found your fence?*

– *No point keeping the necklace. It's not my style.*

He opened the door and stepped inside. There was a dusty, damp staircase straight ahead. It creaked as Ricky climbed it. On the dingy first-floor landing there was a half-open door. Ricky stepped into the room to find a wooden counter, about three metres long, with a brass bell sitting on the top. Behind the counter, four old men sat at desks on very low stools, so that their heads were only a few centimetres above the table tops. They all had eyeglasses attached to one eye, and were examining gemstones and other precious objects. None of them even flinched when Ricky rang the bell, let alone turned round to look at him.

Instead, from a room to the left of the counter, a small, sour-faced old man emerged. He reminded Ricky of Hunter, only older. The old man looked Ricky up and down, as though he were something very unpleasant.

'What do you want, kid?'

'Are you Randolph?'

'I said, what do you want?'

Ricky took the necklace out of his pocket and

placed on the table. If he hadn't been looking carefully at the old man's face, he would have missed the slight widening of his eyes. It told Ricky that the necklace truly was valuable.

The old man made to take it, but Ricky was faster. He grabbed the necklace back up from the counter.

'*Are* you Randolph?' he repeated.

The old man nodded.

'I want to sell the necklace,' Ricky said.

Randolph shrugged. 'It's just costume jewellery, son. I'll give you fifty quid.'

Ricky didn't reply. He dropped the necklace back into his pocket and turned towards the door.

'All right, son,' Randolph said quickly. 'A thousand quid, take it or leave it.'

Ricky continued walking towards the door.

'Ten grand, final offer.'

Ricky stopped, turned and walked back to the counter. 'Cash?' he said.

'Cash.'

He waited as Randolph removed a thick wad of notes from under the counter. Licking his finger, the old man peeled off ten thousand pounds' worth of crumpled, dirty twenty-pound notes. Ricky counted them carefully as they piled up on the desk, surprised by what a small pile such a large amount of money made. Randolph put the money in a paper envelope and Ricky tucked it into the inside pocket of his jacket, then handed over the necklace.

They didn't exchange any more words. Just a brief nod, then Ricky hurried back down the stairs and out into the snowy streets.

He felt on edge carrying such a lot of money around. This was all he had. To lose it would be a disaster.

Izzy Cole spent the rest of the day huddled in the same seat on a Circle Line train. She lost count of the number of times it orbited London. She was too busy staying warm, and keeping her mind off the night that was to come.

At 11:30 p.m., the train terminated at Edgware Road and Izzy shuffled out of the station into the dark, unwelcoming street above. It was as cold as she could ever remember it being. So cold that a tiny part of her mind even considered going back home. But she quickly rejected that idea. Home was where the monsters were.

She tramped up Edgware Road, moving quickly to keep warm. She soon reached Marble Arch, where she turned left to walk down Oxford Street. The Christmas lights were still shining brightly, and the road was crammed with night buses. She chose one at random, paid her fare to the end of the line and found a seat at the very back. Her seat was next to a middle-aged, balding man who smelled faintly of alcohol. He was reading an early edition of the following day's newspaper. Izzy found her eyes wandering towards it.

She froze.

The front page of the paper was taken up by a picture of her father.

Her blood seemed to pump a little harder as she read the article underneath the photograph.

Prominent Tory MP Jacob Cole was today arrested on six counts of terrorism. It is not known if the shooting of a man at the Happy Valley Café is connected to the arrest, but several eye-witnesses report having seen Cole in the vicinity yesterday morning . . .

Izzy snapped her eyes away. She couldn't read any more. A wave of nausea coursed through her, and her head felt as though it had split in two. One half spun horribly with the news of her father. *Six counts of terrorism?* She knew he was a bad man, but what had he really been involved in? The other half of her head grappled with the news that someone had been shot at the café.

Had that someone been Ricky? Was he dead? *Was that why he hadn't turned up that day?*

She knew then that she had to turn up tomorrow at twelve. Just to see.

She turned her head and looked out of the bus window. Everything was blurry because her eyes were filling with tears.

By the time morning came, Izzy had travelled the night bus route three times. Now she had arrived back at Trafalgar Square. She was very hungry and totally exhausted. Red-eyed and footsore, her limbs aching and her muscles crying out for sleep, she walked up towards Piccadilly again.

She had no more money for another tube ticket. She would just have to shelter in the station concourse, and wait.

The morning dragged on slowly. She kept walking round the circular concourse in a kind of daze, hardly knowing what time it was. Each time she passed the newspaper kiosk, she saw her father's face on the front page of all the papers. Soon, her head was a jumble of that image and Ricky's face. Lurking somewhere in the background were her mother's features the last time Izzy had seen her.

You stupid girl, Izzy heard her saying. *You stupid, stupid girl . . .*

Midday. The morning had passed in a blur. Weak with hunger and exhaustion, Izzy stopped ten metres from the newspaper kiosk. A re-run of the previous day. Except today, everyone's faces were a blur. She squinted at passers-by, trying to work out if any of them were Ricky. They gave her very funny looks in return. But none of them were him.

Five minutes past twelve. A dread sickness lurked in the pit of her stomach.

He was dead.

She was truly alone.

She felt the tears coming again. She wanted to scream. To run. To . . .

A hand on her shoulder.

Izzy spun round, her fist clenched. She was ready to hit someone. To protect herself, because from now on she'd need to do that for ever.

Ricky's face stared calmly back at her.

He looked different. Tired, certainly. There were black rings around his eyes and his face was dirty. But there was something else. Ricky looked older. As though, in the day since Izzy had last seen him, he had witnessed things that most people never would. There was a serious frown on his forehead and his eyes were intense. He looked, Izzy thought, slightly scary.

'You're . . . you're alive,' she whispered.

A faint nod as he held up a bandaged hand. 'Just.'

'My father?'

'Prison. A long time. Or so they tell me.'

'Who's "they"?'

Ricky didn't answer.

'What now?' Izzy said.

'You could go home. Your dad won't be there.'

Izzy felt like hissing. Of all people, she thought that Ricky understood. She could never go back to that house, even if it was just her mum there. She took a step backwards, glancing left and right, preparing to run.

'It's up to you, of course,' Ricky said. 'I'm not going to make you do anything.'

'I'm never going home again,' Izzy said. 'Even if I have to live with Hunter and the others—'

'You won't have to,' Ricky interrupted her. He put one hand in his pocket and pulled out a brown envelope, which he handed to Izzy.

She looked inside, then gasped. It was full of banknotes.

'How much . . . ?' she whispered.

'Ten thousand,' he said. 'It's all yours. Find somewhere safe to stay. A room, or a B and B. If you're careful, that should be enough to live on till you turn sixteen. Then maybe you can go be a student or something, start a new life.'

She clutched the envelope hard. 'Where did you get this from?' she breathed.

Ricky sniffed, but for the second time he didn't answer. 'I'm going to go now,' he said. 'But if you ever get into trouble, you can find me here.' He handed Izzy a slip of paper on which he had written the address of the apartment in Docklands.

He held out his hand and Izzy shook it. Then she flung her arms around his neck. 'Thank you,' she whispered. 'For everything.'

Ricky said nothing. Once the hug unfolded he gave her a quick nod. Then he turned and walked away. Seconds later he had melted into the crowd.

Izzy Cole wondered if she would ever see him again.

An hour later, a small, lonely figure stood in the plaza outside a tall apartment block in the Docklands, looking up towards the top floor, his rucksack slung over one shoulder. The snow had started falling again, so heavily this time that all other pedestrians had taken cover inside.

Ricky opened his rucksack and pulled out the letter from his sister. As the blizzard continued to swirl around him, he unfolded the letter and read it:

Dearest Ricky,

I know you won't understand what I'm about to do, but you have to believe me when I say it's for the best. These people they've sent me to live with are the worst. I've got bruises all up my arms and along my back, and I just can't take it any more . . .

Don't be cross with me. And don't forget me. You're a good, clever boy, Ricky. Make sure you do something good and clever with your life. I'm sorry I couldn't do the same.

Love

Madeleine

The wet snow was smudging the ink on the page. Ricky folded up the letter and put it back in his rucksack. Then he looked up to the penthouse again.

A light was on. Someone was home.

Ricky hitched the rucksack over his shoulder again.

— *Are you sure about this?*

— *I'm sure.*

He crossed the plaza, walked into the foyer and called the lift.

It seemed to take an age to carry Ricky to the top floor. As the doors pinged open and he stepped out into the corridor, he saw that the door was open. He stepped towards it, took a deep breath and entered.

Felix was there. He was standing in the main room, looking out of the window across a snow-covered London, his back to Ricky.

'I was only going to give you another couple of hours,' Felix said, still staring out of the window.

Ricky dropped his rucksack on the floor. 'I had a few things to sort out,' he said.

'Obviously.' Felix turned round and took a step towards Ricky. He winced slightly as he put pressure on his prosthetic leg. 'Well?' he asked.

'I want in,' said Ricky. 'Teach me everything.'

The trace of a smile crossed Felix's lips. He turned his back on Ricky and looked back out over London.

'Welcome on board, Agent 22,' he said.

CHRIS RYAN
SAS HERO

- **Joined the SAS in 1984, serving in military hot zones across the world.**

- **Expert in overt and covert operations in war zones, including Northern Ireland, Africa, the Middle East and other classified territories.**

- **Commander of the Sniper squad within the anti-terrorist team.**

- **Part of an 8 man patrol on the Bravo Two Zero Gulf War mission in Iraq.**

- **The mission was compromised. 3 fellow soldiers died, and 4 more were captured as POWs. Ryan was the only person to defy the enemy, evading capture and escaping to Syria on foot over a distance of 300 kilometres.**

- **His ordeal made history as the longest escape and evasion by an SAS trooper, for which he was awarded the Military Medal.**

- **His books are dedicated to the men and women who risk their lives fighting for the armed forces.**

- **You can find Chris on Twitter @exSASChrisRyan**

HAVE YOU READ ALL OF CHRIS RYAN'S ACTION-PACKED FICTION ...?

*'I work for a government agency.
You don't need to know which one ...'*

Meet Agent 21 ...

In a **CODE RED** situation
what would you do . . . ?